A
Piece
is
MISSING

Donald R. Lima

Noble House
Baltimore, Maryland

A Piece Is Missing

Library of Congress
Cataloging in Publication Data
ISBN 1-56167-427-3

Library of Congress Card Catalog Number:
98-85234

Published by

8019 Belair Road, Suite 10
Baltimore, Maryland 21236

Manufactured in the United States of America

Prologue

Prologue

There is an appointed time for everything:
A time to weep, and a time to laugh,
A time to search, and a time to give up as lost.
Eccles. 3:1,4,6

The piece is, I fear, lost. I'm Steven Mack, and this is my story. It is also the story of three women that I loved—Cynthia, Herta, and Anne. They were as different as they were similar. Each meant something different to me, and I loved each in a different way. You will find them to be remarkable women, and perhaps you will love them as I have. This is a story of joy and great sorrow. It is my search for happiness. It addresses the question of how a man, being attracted to an amputee woman might seek to satisfy his attraction. I have quite an adventure bumbling along from place to place. Won't you join me in my quest for the missing piece? Will you please meet . . .

Section One:
Cynthia

Howard Walters bolted upright in his bunk. For an instant he did not even realize that he was awake. His t-shirt was soaked with sweat, much more than usual for this time of year. He realized that he was in a cold sweat. But why? He reached for a cigarette from his fatigue jacket lying on the floor below his bunk, as he swung his feet to the floor.

His buddy in the upper bunk woke up and said, "Hey Howard! It's still dark out and it's Sunday, what are you doing awake?"

"I . . . don't know."

"Is there something wrong?"

"I don't know that either. I just woke up in a cold sweat. I don't recall that ever happening before."

"Is there anything wrong at home?

"Not that I know of. I wish we weren't still on restriction this weekend. I could be with Cynthia."

"You just saw her last weekend, you are surely not worried about her are you?"

"No! There is no reason for this sweat that I know of," Howard replied. "I wish I knew where I was going. Cynthia and I are delaying our wedding plans until it's settled just where the Army is going to send me."

"You really love her don't you, Howard?"

"Yes, Cynthia is really a wonderful girl. We're planning to have a raft of children."

By this time, Howard's cigarette was down to finger level and he threw it in the butt can and crawled back into his bunk. It was Easter Sunday morning, 1954.

The previous day, Cynthia Little had left the Capital City YWCA and boarded a local bus, headed for a visit with Gloria Walters, her future mother-in-law. She had received a phone call from Gloria on Wednesday afternoon asking her to tea. The Walters' were quite influential people in Capital City and she was a little apprehensive about the meeting, as well she might be. To this point she had not received any reaction from Howard's family in regards to the marriage, and she wanted to get a feel for what their thoughts might be.

Howard and Cynthia had already talked about what his parents might say, and they decided that there was nothing that their parents could say or do. It was Howard and Cynthia's decision and it was nobody else's business. If only Howard would be allowed to stay in the United States. If he did not stay States-side, it would be difficult for her. She really wanted him with her. If only he could stay at Concord or be sent to Fort Patton, that would be just great. She thought of these things as she left the bus. She limped slightly as she headed for the Walters' home. She thought about the fact that Howard had only been drafted three weeks ago.

The Walters' home was a very fashionable place. It spoke of money; not millions, mind you, but it was the home of a well-to-do and influential family of Capital City. Mr. Walters was a highly successful business man and his family was one of the most respected within the community and the Catholic Diocese.

Cynthia moved up the stairs and rang the doorbell. The door opened, and Gloria Walters stood before her. She was not a giant by any means; however, she was about five feet seven inches and had a large build. She had dishwater blonde hair which was immaculately kept. Her whole appearance and manner was one of charm and dignity. She was a Walters through and through.

She smiled pleasantly and said, "Oh, hello Cynthia, I'm so glad that you could come. I'm so sorry that we haven't had an opportunity to talk before this." Mrs. Walters added with a slight smile, "Howard speaks so much about you that I almost feel as though I know you. Come let's sit in the living room. I'll bring the tea."

Cynthia gazed around the room as she waited for Mrs. Walters. It was a beautiful room with several lovely paintings on the walls.

"Thank you, I am so glad that you invited me."

"Do you think that you will marry soon?" asked Mrs. Walters. "I mean, after all, Howard is in the Army, and God only knows what they will do with him when he is finished with basic training."

"We want to marry as soon as possible."

"My dear, what's the rush? Perhaps you should wait until after he gets out of the service. Then you could really settle down. My dear child, you are just out of high school. You're just eighteen, aren't you?"

"Yes, but we're so in love and we want to be together—now! Oh, how I do love your Howard."

"Do you plan to have children?" Gloria asked, trying to force a smile. " I mean, do you think it wise?" Gloria's face grew grim as she spoke.

"What business is this of yours whether or not we have children? Are you worried that I would not be able to take care of them properly?"

"Most certainly not. You know very well that it is not the reason for the question. I understand from Howard that your condition is of a congenital nature. Is it not?"

"Yes," replied Cynthia quietly.

"And is it hereditary?"

"What difference does that make to you?"

"Cynthia, could you really bring a child into the world . . . like yourself? After all, life must have been hell for you all these years hasn't it?"

"That's quite an assumption on your part! Yes, I have had my difficulties. I am beginning to know what discrimination in the work place is, but, Mrs. Walters, believe it or not, I've had such wonderful and understanding parents all this time to help me through the rough spots. You have no idea how many wonderful experiences I have had in life, not even including meeting Howard. Life a hell for me, Mrs. Walters? Hardly! I couldn't imagine life for me any other way. Life is, after all, as you know it, to answer your question. No one knows whether or not my condition is hereditary. Perhaps some of our children might be less than physically perfect. Tell me, Mrs. Walters, have you ever met a perfect human being? I thought not. I've given this matter a good deal of thought, Mrs. Walters. I am sure that it would not be difficult for you to believe that, if one of the children should be born in this manner," she lifted her small right hand, which was only a palm without fingers or thumb, "I would be in a very good position to teach my child to cope with life in the same manner that I have. My experience would be of great benefit to my child. My child would learn to smell the roses. Howard and I want very much to have children, and you can be sure that we will. Let's not be unduly concerned when we really don't know what may happen."

"I just don't know what I'd do if one of my grandchild might be malformed."

"You could try loving the child! I must leave, Mrs. Walters. I really must. Thank you for the tea. I promise I will make you a most happy grandmother some day."

Cynthia lit a cigarette as she left the house. As she boarded the bus she could barely hold back the tears that welled up within her. Oh, damn! she thought.

Steven Rogers Mack pulled his old black Pontiac Coupe through the main gate of the main post at Fort Patton, Missouri and headed for Capital City. He had never been there before, but he felt the need to unwind. Perhaps Steven was a bit more excited about being free to go to the city than might be considered. Steven got a bit high about things that way, and he had never given that fact much thought. He had heard that the city was lively, and, frankly, he was bored. He had just bought the old Pontiac from another soldier, whom he did not know, for a few dollars. It was only a hundred miles up to the city, so he left as soon as he had picked up his pass. He thought to himself that tomorrow was Easter Sunday and he would have to find a place to go to mass.

He thought about how beautiful a site Fort Patton was situated on. He had only been there for three months, but he knew he would like to stay there for the rest of his tour of duty. The woods on the base were to be enjoyed and admired. The streams were loaded with fish. When he first arrived on the base, his room looked out on a large mountain. One day he decided to go mountain climbing. With an early morning start, he was barely able to reach half way up the mountain by three. He knew that dark would come with him on the mountain if he did not start back at once.

When he arrived in the Capital City he found a parking lot across from the YWCA. He parked the car and proceeded to find a place to eat. There were a couple of girls in the restaurant, so he asked them if there was a dance in town on Saturday night. They told him about a very popular ballroom on the second level above a department store, in the middle of town.

He went to the dance and he met a couple of nice girls and their father. They lived in Oakline, Missouri and he went there to visit them on a number of occasions. They had a lot of fun together.

When Steven drove into town, he came alone. He had spent most of his life alone, but things were about to change. What happened in Missouri has been unparalleled at any other time in his life. One reason could be that the Missouri people are so much more friendly than the people out West. But no, there was a great deal more to it than that. These girls were just the beginning. They just had a lot of fun together. The strange thing was that this was one of the most difficult, and stressful times of Steven's life, yet, at the same time, the most fun-filled and exciting time. Steven walked the girls back to the car after the dance and said good night. He parked his car back in the parking across from the YWCA and fell asleep behind the wheel of the car he would soon dub The Black Hotel.

Cynthia, was seated in the parlor of the YWCA. She was alone, for all of the girls were out as usual on Saturday night. She had nothing to do this evening but read, and think about Howard.

How she wished he could come and go to mass with her Easter morning, but she knew that was impossible because the entire unit was on restriction until basic training was over.

Sometimes her dear daddy, as she liked to call him, would escort her on his arm, but her father had to go to Albuquerque for Easter. He was a big and burly man with a red mustache. He was a kind, gentle man and a prominent lawyer. With all of this, he had a good deal of difficulty in accepting Cynthia's problems. He just couldn't. The fact was that he felt a great deal of guilt over Cynthia. No one blamed him, not anyone accept himself. He seemed to have the feeling that it was either his sins or sins of his ancestors being revisited upon him. Raymond Little and Blanche Little divorced when Cynthia was thirteen years old, not long after the event that finally shaped Cynthia's future occurred. Whether or not his unfounded sense of guilt over Cynthia had anything to do with the divorce is a matter of speculation. One thing is certain, however, Cynthia adored her daddy, and he loved her also.

Cynthia put down the book, went over to the piano, and played "Claire De Lune," picking out the melody with her small right hand. As she played, her thoughts strayed to Camp Concord and the life she would have with Howard. She got up, doused the light, and went up to bed.

Cynthia was enjoying the soothing warm water as it pulsed over her small frame. She didn't usually have the luxury of taking a long shower before work, so she got up a little early before mass in order to enjoy one. She had just graduated from high school in June, and wouldn't have her nineteenth birthday until later in the year. She was so pleased that she had a job as a switchboard operator. Getting that job had been a real struggle. She had looked for it for three months. It was her first attempt at getting a job and she had never dreamed that she would face such discrimination. She got really flimsy excuses from prospective employers such as "Our insurance won't cover you," "You may injure yourself," "The position has been filled," and the like. By the end of three month, Cynthia was weary of job hunting. She was appalled, and just plain tired. Even though she was becoming tired, she was not the one to give up. She had heard people telling her what she could and couldn't do all of her life. It was a great relief to finally be working, even at such a meager job, and to be living on her own. She really enjoyed her new found freedom, and sometimes, just sometimes, she wondered if she should really get married?"

Cynthia turned off the shower, grabbed a towel and dried herself, then hopped over to the bed. She sat on the bed, put on her panties, put on her left shoe and stocking. She took the long wool sock from the bed, pulling it over her right knee and up to her thigh. She picked up her leg and slipped her stump into it and fastened it on, as she had for years. She moved to the mirror to look at her small chest, and she wondered why she couldn't at least have been a little better endowed as she fastened her bra. She finished dressing, putting on her silky white blouse and blue skirt. She looked sharp. She limped out of the room and headed for the big Catholic Church just up the hill.

Steven opened his eyes, the sun was getting into them. He looked around and, for the moment, he didn't know where he was, after all he had never slept in the Black Hotel before. He was dressed in his civilian clothes. Who wants to wander around in a monkey suit anyway? He got out of the car, locked it, smoothed his clothes as best he could, and headed for the church on the hill. It was Easter Sunday, and he was late, as usual. There was no place to sit, so he knelt at the back of the church.

Sometime during the early part of the mass he noticed that a woman was stroking the back of her head with what appeared to be a very much too small hand. He more or less forgot about it. The church was very crowded with people. Steven had not gone to confession the previous day, so he couldn't receive communion. When communion time came, the woman he had observed earlier got up and went to the altar. Something which seemed unusual to him at the time happened. She didn't return directly up the aisle to her seat as he expected her to. Instead she came back up the aisle to Steven's right and then passed directly in front of him. It was then that he noticed that she was limping. He looked down and discovered that she was wearing an artificial leg.

Steven didn't know what to think; there was no thinking going on in his mind. He was totally stunned. He felt helpless. It was as if there was something he had to do, but there was nothing! Then the hurt came. He felt as though he had been hit in the stomach with an anvil (a feeling like he had never known before). And confusion, what confusion, but over what he didn't know. He felt a compassion like he had never felt before. His mind was in a rage. He couldn't account for what he was feeling now as his knees felt as though the were glued to the floor. He was so uncomfortable that he tried to think of what to do. His first thought was to run like hell, but he'd look funny bolting out of that big church.

After mass, he lingered a bit before leaving. He waited for her to leave first. She was about his age and she had a nice slender build to her small frame of five feet two inches.

As she left, she did not notice him, so he started to follow her. He didn't know exactly what he was doing, but he felt that he needed to know something more about her, as if that could stop the anxiety that he felt. He followed her, but only until he realized that she was going toward the YWCA. His feet suddenly turned and he veered off toward the center of town. His head was not clear yet and, most assuredly, his brain was not working. He just kept walking.

After a couple of miles of just walking at a rapid pace, he stopped, lit a cigarette and sat on the step of the house behind him. His heart had stopped pounding, and his breathing became easier. He just sat there, almost in a stupor. When he finished his cigarette, he got up and slowly began to retrace his steps. He stopped at a cafe along the way, and was barely able to eat breakfast. After breakfast, he returned to the car.

As soon as he had shut the door the tears began to roll down his cheeks. He cried for what seemed like an hour. He didn't know why. He suddenly realized that a piece of himself was missing. He didn't know which piece it was, and he didn't know where it had gone. He just knew the piece was missing and he had the strangest feeling that he was going to have one hell of a time getting it back. He started the car, took one more look of the YWCA in front of him and headed for Fort Patton.

The phone in the hall was ringing! Cynthia was expecting a call from Howard, and she raced for the phone as quickly as she was could.

"Hello!"

"Hello, Cynthia?"

"Oh, Howard. How are you? I really missed you at mass this morning. I wish that Basic would get over with so that you could come home more often. Oh darling, I miss you so very very much."

"Is everything all right there?"

"Why yes, Howard, everything is just fine. Why do you ask?"

"I woke up this morning in a cold sweat. I've never done that before. I was just looking for a reason for it?"

"Oh Howard! Those things do happen and there isn't usually a reason for them. Well, anyway, I did have a visit with your mother yesterday."

"Oh how nice. I hope she treated you nicely."

"Why shouldn't she? She invited me for tea."

"Oh? What did you talk about?"

"Just a little girl talk, you know how that goes, just small talk, you know. Can we see each other next weekend? You know that I'm planning to come, don't you?"

"You bet I know! I'll meet you at the front gate at noon. You know I love you, darling."

"I know you do, Howard, and I love you so much. I'll call you later on in the week. Keep your chin up honey. Oh, before I forget, do you have any idea when you'll get your orders?"

"I'm not sure, but it should be in about six weeks. Good-bye, darling. I'll talk to you later on this week."

Steven awoke. It was Monday morning. He was becoming baked by the infamous Midwestern heat. Blankets were beginning to disappear from the barracks. When he awoke he had a slight headache, but other than that he felt like he'd gone through a knot-hole. His mouth was dry, and his stomach was queasy. He felt as if he'd either been on a three-day drunk or was pregnant. He concluded that it wasn't the latter. He was still puzzled by this strong reaction to this girl.

Steven was a jeep driver. He had been transferred to Fort Patton from California after basic training. He had gone through cooking school while at Fort Ord and truly hated it. Just because he had been a busboy while in high school they decided to make him cook. Well, during cooking school, he almost never cooked. He was content to be the dining room orderly. What he had really wanted to do was to be an instructor, but there was no way he could get near that job without a degree. Steven was just eighteen and fresh out of high school. He was interested in entertainment. Unfortunately, the only thing he was doing at the time was pantomime, and he wasn't very good at it either. Several professional entertainers were on the base, including a pantomimist. Steven recalled the time that "Ebb Tide" first came out. The first version, without lyrics, was by Frank Chatsfield's Orchestra. Steven wrote a narrative speaking version of lyrics for the song. Before he had a chance to use it at a service club, a version with singing lyrics came out.

Steven had been a tap dancer in high school. Actually, he had taken tap lessons when he was in grammar school. He had always enjoyed it and he missed it at times. There was a boy in high school by the name of Teddy, who was a magnificent tap dancer. Steven didn't know him at all. At the beginning of summer in 1951 Steven called Teddy on the phone and told him that he knew a little about tap and would he be interested in trying to put together a tap dance duo. Teddy said he might be interested and would call Steven later. Teddy was a swell guy. An accomplished pianist and into composing serious music, he was some kind of a genius. He was slightly built and as graceful as a cat at times.

Teddy called Steven the next day and asked to meet him at the band stand in the park at nine o'clock the next morning. Steven parked his Model-A and noticed that Teddy had a girl with him. He recognized her immediately. It was Janet, an old friend from his drama teacher's stage crew. All three of them were interested in the theatre, Teddy less than Janet and Steven.

Teddy said, straight out, "Steven, Janet doesn't have any dancing experience. She told me some time ago that she'd like to learn to dance."

They worked hard all summer. They worked two or three hours a day and had great fun with it. The venture was successful, and they danced in the opening day assembly at school. Shortly after, Steven tried to go it alone and wound up falling on his head. The reason he hadn't tried to dance at Fort Ord was that he just couldn't put a routine together. Teddy left school during his senior year to get married.

Steven picked up his jeep. He was to take the colonel out to the field for field firing observation. He still felt a bit in a daze. He just wasn't himself. He moved the jeep toward the colonel's home. He recalled that when he first came to Fort Patton he was assigned to a unit as part of the cooking staff. He immediately volunteered to be a dining room orderly.

His offer was taken up forthwith. The only good thing about being a member of the cooking staff was that he was first in the chow line and got every other day off. During his time in the service Steven had a knack for getting jobs with reduced hours.

Things went along pretty well until the regular mess sergeant came back from leave. He had separate rations and he was supposed to live off post. Apparently, he'd had a domestic quarrel with his wife. At any rate, he decided to stay in the cook's room. He further decided that Steven was going to sleep on the floor, and he was going to sleep in Steven's bunk. He was a very physically powerful person and Steven was, frankly, afraid of him. He just couldn't argue with this sergeant.

Steven was learning to adjust to the Army. Sometimes he learned the hard way. Every payday this barracks turned into a gambling casino. For the first two months Steven lost all his money on payday evening. It was a hard lesson, but he was never broke again during the rest of his time in the Army. He banked part of his money every payday, and was disappointed that they didn't have a bank at his next post.

Finally Steven, was assigned as a cook on a regular shift, and he was to start the next morning at four. That night, some of the boys drank a little peach brandy. Steven got more than his share that evening and never made his shift. As a matter of fact, Steven never pulled one shift as a cook in his whole stay in the service. After a couple of days the commanding officer called him into his office. He was very nice to Steven, and he wasn't a bit angry with him. He told him that he knew about some of the problems he had and offered him a transfer. Steven was elated. As soon as he was transferred, the new company commander asked him what he wanted to do. Steven said he'd like to be a jeep driver. The captain said, "Wish granted!" End of Steven's problems? Oh, hell no!

Cynthia slipped out the front door of the Y and moved quickly toward the department store where she worked. She was proud of her job there, even as a switchboard operator. It meant independence. It meant freedom from the ranch. She had spent most of her life on a ranch, and, frankly, that was just no place for her. She was happy as she moved along street, she had Howard, and he was something.

She had never had a boyfriend in her life. The fact that Howard wanted to marry her, and he being only her first boyfriend, sent tingles up her spine. Yet sometimes she wondered if she was really ready to give up this new and challenging life she had fought so hard to gain. Was she ready to settle down to a married life, without really struggling, without fully testing her abilities, which her parents worked so hard to provide her with the opportunity to gain. It seemed to her that dropping out before she really had a chance to accomplish anything would be a sin. She was not really sure yet, but it would take an awful lot to make her abandon Howard.

She couldn't help but think about Mrs. Walters' conversation with her on Saturday. She was disappointed in the fact that Mrs. Walters had such strong concerns about the marriage. As for Cynthia, she was going to pray for God's help. She knew that the matter was out of her hands, and that only through him could her children be perfectly formed. Cynthia reached the department store, and the gate guard let her pass.

That afternoon as she was answering calls. "The department store. How may I help you?"

"Hello, Cynthia?" She recognized Gloria's voice, and wished she hadn't.

"Oh, Mrs. Walters, how are you? How may I direct your call?"

"No, I wanted to talk to you, dear. I'm afraid that I behaved badly Saturday and I wanted to apologize for it. Will you accept it?"

"Why yes, of course. I'm sure it was just a misunderstanding," Cynthia said. What else could she say? This was not the time or place for her to vent her true feelings.

"Are you going to Camp Concord this weekend, dear?"

"Of course, you know that the boys are all on restriction until basic training is over. I want to be with Howard as much as possible."

"By the way, dear, have you and Howard . . . yet?"

"Have we what, Gloria? Planned the wedding?"

"Why, uh, yes, exactly. Say hello to Howard for me I'll talk to you later Cynthia," she said as she furrowed her brow, and wondered how she might stop the wedding.

Cynthia took a moment before she answered another call. They most certainly hadn't been together, but what business was it of hers. Cynthia was angry.

Steven was off from work for the day. He got into his old Pontiac and headed for one of the auxiliary service clubs and perhaps a chance to relax with a game of pool. He just couldn't get that girl out of his mind. She was so lovely. When he thought of her, questions came to him like spears. More questions came to him than he had ever thought of in his life. How could God have let this happen to anyone, let alone this lovely girl? Perhaps she'd had an accident. But no, Steven didn't think so. He had watched her as she crossed the street, and she did not act at all as if she had any fear moving among the cars. Steven thought that she was about his age. Where in the hell would he be if he had a body like hers to carry through life?

He had turned the motor off in front of the service club. He could hear the sound of a piano coming from within. That music, although he didn't know it at the time, was to usher in one of the most exciting and gratifying experiences of his life, even if things didn't all workout just perfectly.

He entered the club and saw a rather large young man of twenty-two or twenty-three playing the piano. In the middle, up on the stage, a man and woman were singing a number from *Kiss Me Kate*. Everyone was dressed in civilian clothes, except for a few who were in costume. This was obviously a rehearsal of some kind. He forgot about the pool game and sat down to watch.

Steven talked to one of the cast and discovered that they were going to present the music of *Kiss Me Kate* in the main service club in two weeks. Steven was enjoying himself watching. These entertainers were real pros. They were also, as you will see, quite a diverse group of people. The one thing the group could really do together was to put on a show.

As the evening progressed, Steven discovered that the cast was short one member. A comedy number was supposed to be sung by two gunmen, but at the time they had only one gunman. Steven raised his hand and suggested that he might take a crack at it. He did that before he looked at the words. The song had five versus to it, and the words were totally impossible. Steven tried and he tried. He learned two versus by the time the show went on. Steven thought it would be nice to add in a little tap number, with no objections heard from the rest of the cast. By show's opening, things were in fair shape and the dance routine was working well. They rehearsed through Friday.

By 7:30 Saturday morning Cynthia had hustled around the corner and gotten in line to purchase her ticket to Howard's base. She boarded the bus and selected a seat in the smoking section in the back. She was very excited about seeing Howard, as it had been almost a month since they were together.

She had met Howard this past June at her graduation party

at the Shados Hill Amusement Park. It was about ten, and she'd been riding with the gang since six. She had just come off the park's roller coaster.

She was feeling a bit tired and suddenly she noticed that there was no one around. She decided to slip out into a little wooded area all by herself. As she moved in, she noticed a bench built onto a tree. She sat down and lit a cigarette. She just settled back and relaxed. There was a nice, warm, comfortable breeze, and she was just beginning to enjoy it. Suddenly she heard the footsteps of someone running toward her. Soon a guy came trotting past her. When he was three steps beyond her, he turned his head. He saw Cynthia and stopped dead in his tracks

"Oh, hello, there! I almost didn't see you," he said as he walked back toward her. "I don't believe I've ever seen you before. Are you with the graduation group?"

"Yes, I am" she smiled. She did like his looks, and she thought him a bit on the debonair side.

"I graduated two years ago. A couple of my buddies and I decided to check your class out. My name's Howard." He extended his hand to shake.

Cynthia's heart sank. She knew she wanted to shake hands. She could feel a bead of sweat break on her brow. Ordinarily with people who knew her, or knew something about her, it was no problem, but she knew that Howard had only seen her in the dark. She thought to offer him her left hand, which was very coarse from all the extra work it had been forced to do over the years, but she had not offered her left hand in a handshake in many years.

"My name is Cynthia and no one calls me Cindy—except my Daddy," she said as she extended her little hand.

Howard noticed it for the first time as he took it, oh so gently in his, looked into her eyes, smiled, and said, "I'm very pleased to meet you, too."

"My full name is Cynthia Little."

"My full name is Howard Walters."

Cynthia suggested, "You come from a rather well-known family. Isn't your father a well known financier?"

"Well, I don't know about that, but isn't your father Big Red Little, the attorney?"

"Why yes, but how did you know?"

"Well in case you weren't aware of it, your father packs a real wallop in this town. What school are you planning to go to?"

"I'm not going to school, at least not right away."

"Well why not? Surely your parents have enough money, don't they?"

"Oh! It's not that. There's something I've got to do first." Then she said, "I'd better get back to the party." She rose and preceded Howard to the park.

He quickly caught up with her and walked along side her. "I'd like to see you again, Do you think that's possible?" Howard was saying as they reached the lights of the park. Then Howard noticed for the first time that Cynthia was wearing an artificial leg. A big warm grin came over her face. He couldn't know about the glow that was heating the inside of her with ecstasy.

She replied, "I'm moving into the YWCA tomorrow. I'll be looking for my first job. Here is my number, give me a call." She handed him the piece of paper she had fished out of her purse and written her number on. Then she went off to find her ride home.

As he ran off toward his friends, Howard called out, "Hey Cynthia, I'm a Catholic. What are you?"

The words hit her eardrum and her heart did the thump thump. She responded, "I'm Catholic too, but only for two months." Then she added, "Good night, Howard."

Then she felt an earthquake, and she shook her eyes open. The bus driver smiled down on her and said, "Last stop, this is Camp Concord, you don't want to keep that soldier boy waiting do you?" She looked at him, smiled, and shook her head.

Howard was standing at the gate as she left the bus. She saw him, and just ran!

On a pleasantly warm Saturday afternoon, Steven returned to the barracks after motor stables. He put on his civilian clothes and picked up his pass from the orderly room. He walked out to his car, when he was about two feet away he stopped just for a moment. He knew that he couldn't stop wanting to meet her. He really didn't know what he could do. He got into the car, and pointed it for Capital City.

As he drove, he tried to keep his mind on the show. He thought about the people in the show. He was finding the workings of the group fascinating. If you knew the people, individually, you would think that they were most unlikely to pull together as a team. There were three women in the group Jane, Helen, and Sharon. They were excellent singers. Steven never became well acquainted with them. There were five men other than Steven in the show. His partner was a young, tall, round faced, red head by the name of Charles. Chuck had just a little more talent than Steven did. Then there was a tall black fellow with a beautiful tenor voice. He didn't hesitate to claim that he was an Indian. He rode with Steven to the city sometimes. There was another excellent singer who rode with him sometimes, too. He was a homosexual. These three were a part of the show, but they were not a part of Steven's gang.

Jamie was an Army lieutenant from the Midwest assigned temporary duty at Fort Patton for artillery training. Michael was a Marine lieutenant from Chicago, also on temporary duty at Fort Patton. The three of them formed a close friendship during the show, and Steven was very grateful to them.

He parked The Black Hotel (his Pontiac) across from the YWCA and set out to supper. Very little occurred during this trip. He went to the dance that night.

The next morning he went to the nine o'clock mass. Then he went to the ten o'clock mass. Cynthia was nowhere to be seen. That afternoon, he decided to go to a dance the girls at the Y put on for the soldiers every Sunday. He stayed and danced a while. He enjoyed dancing, and some of the girls were very good.

After a long while a thought occurred to him. He really didn't know if she lived here or not. He left the dance and found a house mother. He suddenly became embarrassed, and was sure that he was sticking his nose where it really didn't belong. Some how he managed to say, "Excuse me miss but a . . ." He was stumbling.

"Why yes, may I help you?"

"Could you tell if a certain girl lives here?"

"If she does, I suppose I could," she said with a gentle smile. He felt a little more confident. He described the girl in church to her. She smiled with delight and said, "Why yes, she does. She's not in right now, but I think she'll be in this evening."

With that Steven began to back slowly away, then he turned and walked swiftly away from her. As he did, he heard her say, "She's been engaged for about three months now." What he didn't hear her say was, "Would you like to meet her?"

Steven crossed to his car, got in, and headed for the Fort. He was angry. He wasn't angry at the lady, or anyone else. He was angry at himself. How had he given up his self control? He couldn't shake the feeling he got from just seeing her. There had been several girls he had forgotten after one date. On the other hand, there had been several girls who had forgotten him after one date also. What difference can it really make? She's engaged. Then Steven thought, what does being engaged have to do with it, anyway?

He pulled the car off the road, locked it up, and started walking slowly across an open field. He stopped and grabbed a handful of dirt. Then it occurred to him, could it be, was it remotely possible that Steven was in love with her? How could he know? He had never felt this way before. Never had he ever been in love. How helpless he felt. He could make a fool of himself, and yet there was such a thirst which no fountain could quench. He must forget about this, he decided. It made no since at all. But how could he? Such a strong image of her lie within his head. Yet, he feared not only for himself, but also for her. He would not hurt her for the world, yet if he were to contact her, who knew in what way she might be hurt? If it was truly love, then all things must be respected. He was petrified. The only thing he could do was not return to the city, just to let her be. "Oh yes! That must be the solution," he told himself.

He hurried back to his car and returned to the base.

Howard and Cynthia had supper at the enlisted men's mess. Howard wished that he could take Cynthia out on the town for supper, but Cynthia didn't mind it at all. She was just glad she could be with Howard. She really wished that they could be alone, but she knew they couldn't. They had a pleasant two days, but Howard was quite concerned about the orders which would soon come. He told Cynthia that he was concerned that they might ship him to Korea because many of the troops leaving were going there.

"Oh, well," he said, "we'll know in about two weeks."

Cynthia hoped that she hid the fear that penetrated her body. "Don't worry, Howard, everything will be all right." Oh, Lord, Cynthia thought, please let this be so. You know how I love him, Lord, I wouldn't tell anyone but you, Lord, but I need him so. Please don't take my love from me!

Howard walked Cynthia to the bus and watched her board. She reminded him, "Howard, don't forget that I'm going to the ranch to visit Mother next weekend."

"Yes, I know. I wish I could go with you. Just stay off Old Blue, won't you?"

"Yes, love, I will." Howard took her in his arms and held her for the longest time, then they kissed. Cynthia brushed back a tear, and boarded the bus. She went back to her usual smoking seat, and pressed her nose to the window until Howard was out of sight. Cynthia settled back, lit a cigarette and relaxed. She thought back to a night just four months ago.

Cynthia and Howard had gone to a movie, and afterward they had picked up a couple of beers and found a place to park. They were chitchatting along about the movie and about things in general, when Howard put his beer down, took her hands in his and gently said, "Will you marry me, Cynthia?"

Fortunately it was dark and she could barely see the outline of his face. She hoped he didn't see hers. Her face grew pale and grim. A cloud of fear crossed over her like none she had ever felt. God she loved him. She loved him more than her own self, but she wasn't sure of him, not yet.

"Uh uh, what did you say Howard?"

"I said, will you be my wife?"

"Right now I don't know, Howard." She tightened her grip on his hand. "There are a lot of things we haven't talked about," she said, striving to remain calm.

"Like what, for instance?" Howard earnestly asked.

"Well, for one thing, my artificial limbs are very expensive."

"Gee, I hadn't thought about that, but I'm sure that we can manage that somehow, don't you?"

"What about children, Howard? Do you want to have children?"

"Oh sure, lots of them. Don't you?"

"Yes, I really do. Please forgive me for not talking about this before, but I really wasn't expecting your proposal."

"Well, Cynthia what are you talking about?"

"My physical problems stem from a congenital condition. I am the only one in the family that has it that we know of, but the doctors do not know what caused the defect. There is a possibility that one or more of our children might have the same problem."

Howard, put his arms around Cynthia, drew her close to him, and he remained silent for a very, very long time. He closed his eyes and he almost wept. He pulled Cynthia's face next to his and he whispered in her ear, "Cynthia, I love you," then, after a long pause, "We'll face this problem together."

Cynthia was all joy now, but there was still a problem and she just couldn't answer yet. "I'll give you an answer on our date next Saturday, okay?"

Howard wrinkled his brow in puzzlement. "Fine," he said.

By this time he was at the Y and she got out of the car, gave him a big kiss, and headed up to her room.

Cynthia was beginning to doze off, there on the bus, but her thoughts and recollections remained clear and accurate. The next day on her first work break she had called her dearest and closest friend, Andrea and asked her a favor. At first, Andrea didn't understand, but she did by the end of the conversation. It really didn't matter to Andrea, for she and Cynthia were very close, and she would do any thing for her. On Wednesday,

Cynthia received an envelope which contained a ring of keys in the mail. She slipped the keys into her purse and went up to her room. She thought that she really didn't want to do this and she didn't know how it would effect Howard, but she had faced so many rejections before in her life, that she knew that she had to take the chance now. She had been misunderstood so many times. So many times had things happened to her that were so painful she just had go to her bed and hide herself under the covers because she felt so isolated and alone. She just wanted to escape. Oh how she had cried to herself, "Why me, Lord? Oh, my God, why me? Why anyone? Oh, to just be able to escape this body if, only for one hour. Who knows how it is never to have walked a single step on my own two feet in my entire lifetime." If that were not enough, then also, to suffer the slings and arrows of persecution from the ignorant. The glances and the stares to which she is never completely immune, even though she knows that ninety-eight percent of the people meant no harm. They just didn't know what to say or do. She did truly understand that. She had made it a habit to use her hands, and never to hide them. She hid them sometimes, but only when she was aware of someone staring for too long a time. With Howard, she knew he wanted her, and she knew it with certainty, but they would live a long time together, and if she can be more certain of him now, they will both be happier in the long run.

Howard called that evening and Cynthia told him that she would meet him in front of the Y at three o'clock Saturday.

Cynthia stirred a moment, looked out the bus window, and settled back to her half-conscious thoughts.

At three o'clock Cynthia was standing on the curb when Howard drove up. Cynthia kissed him through the open window and went around and got in. Howard pulled away from the curb.

Cynthia said, "Please drive to the corner of Garnet and Brown."

Howard gave her a puzzled look, and did as she asked. Cynthia was very quiet, which was unusual for her.

"OK, Howard turn left down Garnet Street. See that white

house? Pull into the driveway."

"What?"

"It's all right, honey. This place belongs to my very best friend's parents, there's nobody home."

Howard got out of the car, as Cynthia fished the keys out of her purse and opened the gate. Howard came up as the gate came open, revealing a large swimming pool.

Cynthia said, "The men's dressing room is over there. You'll find a new pair of trunks lying on the bench for you, now go on!"

Cynthia entered the women's dressing room, knelt before the bench, which wasn't very easy for her., and said an Our Father and three Hail Mary's, then, "Please, Father, let this be possible, I love him so. Oh! Father please."

She removed her clothes and put on the one piece bathing suit with shoulder straps. She removed her leg and took under her arms the pair of crutches leaning on the wall of dressing room. She walked to the door, paused, took a deep breath, and walked out on the pool deck.

Howard was sitting in the water on the shallow edge of the pool. When he saw her standing there, he slowly got out of the pool and walked over to her. He put his arms around her waist, pulling her body to his, and as he did she threw her arms around his neck, letting the crutches fall to the deck.

"Cynthia, I love you, my dear, and I want you for my wife. Now give your answer!"

"Yes!" she said, her heart pounding. "Oh, yes and please soon."

Her body suddenly became hot and her breathing grew rapid. She could feel Howard's hard penis pressing against her thigh through his trunks. He held her tighter, and kissed her, oh so passionately, and she knew there was no other man in the world like Howard. She took her arms from around his neck and hopped back a short step. She dropped the straps of her bathing suit and took hold of the top of it and slid it to the deck. Howard lifted her and she kicked the suit to the dressing room door. She pulled the string of his bathing suit lose and slid it down his legs. He stepped out of it. He lifted her and pressed her breasts against his hairy chest as he gently rubbed her bare buttocks. She could feel his strong hot penis pressing against her. He rubbed her gently with his hand.

Finally she said, "I'm losing control." She took hold of his penis, put her arm around his neck, and they embraced. She hopped one step back, turned around, hopped another step and dove into the pool. She swam to the middle of the pool, rolled over onto her back, and floated with her thighs spread, and she was a beautiful sight indeed, to Howard, who sat on the edge of the pool and watched her. She closed her eyes and just relaxed. The Missouri sun pleasantly baking her. Finally, Howard got into the water and waded out to her.

She said, "I'm sorry, I didn't want this to happen." She was almost in tears. "I had to bring you here. I had to!"

"Yes, I know, and I'm glad you did, we both know that there won't be any surprises now. Nothing is hurt by what happened here."

Cynthia swam back over to the edge of the pool, pulled herself up on the edge, took her crutches and walked to her dressing room, shouting at the top of her lungs, "Yes! Yes! Yes!"

"Yes, what? This is Capital City," said the bus driver, as he shook her.

"Yes, thank you, driver," she said as she prepared to leave the bus.

Steven was still wrestling with the problem on Wednesday when he picked up his jeep and headed for the colonel's quarters. He was deep in thought when suddenly his left front tire hit a wet spot in the road and he lost control of the jeep. It slid over against the right curb, bending the wheel and axle. Steven got out and looked. There sure wasn't any way to slide this one under the table. It reminded him of the time he was trying to lay rubber with his Model A and the axle broke, only then he had his dad and one of his dad's friends, who drove the truck with him, to help fix it. But now, oh! Who was going to help him now?

He wobbled the jeep back to the motor pool and filled out

the accident report. When the captain saw the report, he blew a fuse. He was so angry that he could have spit.

After taking a few minutes to cool off, he said to his first lieutenant, "Oh, hell, we just won't mention this." The captain wasn't sure just why he said it, and later he did have reason to regret it. He handed the first lieutenant some papers and said, "Here, give him these on Friday."

Steven didn't hear another thing about the incident for a very long time, which gave him cause to wonder.

Rehearsals were going well. They had built a platform for a stage, which covered a third of the dance hall in the main service club. In a week the show would open. Steven felt a bit relieved that at last the show would finally open. He was still struggling with the words to "Brush Up Your Shakespeare," but felt a bit more comfortable than he had.

He was determined not to return to Capital City, perhaps not ever. He decided that it was time to get away alone for a quiet weekend.

On Friday, the lieutenant delivered to Steven the papers the captain had given him. Steven couldn't believe his eyes. They were orders to deuce and a half (two and one half ton truck) school. With great relief at not getting into a scrape, Steven picked up his pass at noon on Saturday. He had noticed a small town about halfway between Fort Patton and the big city, a town by the name of Farmertown. He arrived about 1:30 in the afternoon. The small town had one side street for businesses, and the bus depot was the only building on the main thoroughfare. Just to make the small town smaller, it was also the best place in town to eat. He pulled the car to a stop next to the station. He knew he didn't want to stay in the Black Hotel. He asked a waitress about a place to stay, and she told him about the house directly across the street.

He went immediately over and rented a room. He walked around town, exploring it all in less than ten minutes, and then walked a mile or two down the road. He knew that there was a dance in town every Saturday night, and he planned to attend. When he returned to his room, he took a short nap. When he woke he prayed. "Thank you, God, for help in getting away from the city." He had finally found strength to deal with the situation and hoped it would soon be in the forgotten past.

About 5:15 he got up, washed, and walked over the bus station to have dinner. There were several old wooden stairs leading up into the station. He seated himself at the counter and ordered a T-bone steak. He looked the room over as he waited. There was an average sized woman, dressed in black slacks and a white blouse, seated in one corner of the station. She had coal black hair.

Cynthia rounded the corner from the Y carrying a small case. It was 4:15 when she handed the bus driver her ticket stamped Farmertown and climbed on the bus. She was going to the ranch, she was going home, and only to visit!

The waitress presented Steven with his steak. At that moment a bus pulled up out front. Steven began to eat his steak as he casually looked out toward the bus, and in that instant he noticed someone with a limp coming toward the station. Steven fixed his gaze on the station door. In a moment the person, a woman, stood not more than thirty feet from him. It wasn't just, a woman, it was . . . her. Steven's mouth fell open. He wasn't staring or glaring, he was transfixed, He couldn't move. He tried to drink a glass of water, but he spilled most of it on himself. He needed a cooling off by this time, anyway. Now the woman with the black hair had her arm around the young lady from the bus and they left, before Steven was anywhere near able to get up. Steven finished his steak as best he could, but his hands were trembling and he could hardly fumble the money out of his pocket to pay the bill.

As he left the station he knew that his life had just changed, even though he did not yet understand at all what that signified. As he realized what had happened, and how his prayers had been so strangely answered, not only was he excited, he had a feeling of total exhilaration beyond any he could remember. The person, he had feared to try to meet, had been brought to

him. There had to be a reason, and he intended to find out.
Cynthia enjoyed the ten mile ride from Farmertown to Mom's
ranch.

Mother spoke, "Well, how do like being up in the big city
alone?"

"I just love it, Mom. The only thing I'm really going to
miss when Howard and I marry will be the independence and
freedom I have now. Mama, I waited so long for the day when
I could feel and know without anyone else interfering, that I
could live alone and take care of myself. Oh, I knew it, there
was no doubt, but I had to do it myself. Had I gotten married
without being at least a little while alone, I could never have
lived a life which is full. I really wish that Howard wouldn't
have come along as quickly as he did. I would have liked to
have had a chance to grow a bit more and enjoy. You know,
Mama, he's just a wonderful man."

"Has he gotten his orders, honey?"

"No, but I think that it will be very soon. I'm really praying
over that. You be sure to pray also, won't you, Mama? If he
were to be shipped overseas I think I would break the
engagement."

"Why, Cynthia?"

"Well, it's like I said, having him gone would be too
constraining. I just wouldn't want that kind of pressure. It would
be better to be able to continue the way things are now. This
freedom is a fresh breeze in my face. Mama, I just can't turn
my back on it."

"I know, darling. I'm very proud of you!"

"Mama, if it wasn't for you, what would have happened to
me? If you hadn't fought and scraped for the things you knew
were right for me, I wouldn't be where I am today. How can I
ever thank you or repay you, Mama?"

Blanche smiled and put her arm around her daughter's
shoulder, and the car found its way to the back of the ranch
house and stopped.

Steven had been praying all week that God would give him the strength to stick to his resolve to forget that girl. Steven was doing what he could, in order to do what he knew he must. He hadn't tried for very long. Now God had given him a very clear and direct answer. Steven must now seek her. Steven knew that there was something very important to his life in a meeting with that girl. He got down on his knees and prayed to the Lord that he might understand what was going on. It was a certainty that he soon would be in Capital City again.

Steven went to the dance that evening, and he almost enjoyed himself. The next morning, when he awoke, took a shower, and returned to the base he was still in the state of ecstasy. He almost flew home on wings of joy.

Cynthia loved to ride. Her stepfather had saddled her horse for her before she got up. Her mother had fixed her a quick snack for breakfast, knowing that Cynthia would be anxious to get going. She came through the kitchen, said good morning, picked up the egg sandwich snack, and went out the back door almost without stopping. Cynthia mounted her horse and started down the path at a trot.

She was sorry that she had to miss church that morning, but she needed this visit with her mother. Her father was a Catholic, but her mother was a Southern Baptist. She had lived with her mother during most of her teen years, after her mother and father divorced when she was thirteen. She had had little peace attending her mother's church. She started looking into Roman Catholicism, independent of her father's urging, although she sat and talked to him by the hour about it before she decided to become a Catholic. This decision gave Cynthia a new peace from within.

She must have ridden for three hours. She wished that Howard were there. As she thought of him, she sent up a little prayer for their future together. She was concerned. She just couldn't lose him now.

Cynthia was back at the house a while later. It was almost time for the bus back to the city. Later that evening, she packed her bag and her mother took her to the station.

When she got back to Capital City, Howard called and, during the conversation, told her that he had the sweats again. Cynthia was concerned. The last time was Easter morning. She assured Howard that there was nothing to worry about. She worried a bit anyway, even though there was no apparent reason.

Cynthia went up to bed. What had the house mother told her last week? Someone wanted to meet her? Oh well, she thought as she readied herself for bed, I don't see a thing to worry about. She slid into bed, rolled over, and fell into a deep sleep.

It was Monday morning, and Steven was to start driving school. He was physically and mentally tired, as the events of the weekend had left him flattened. That didn't bode well for him. He had to drive only once or twice in a two hour period during school. The rest of the time he laid down in the back of the truck and tried to catch up on his rest, for he had a sickly headache.

By Wednesday, he was feeling much better. That was fortunate because the show opened that night. It was an exciting night for the whole cast, but the evening was not without its surprises. Steven's partner and he had nailed down a little more than two stanzas of their song. A little over half way through the show they came down the aisle carrying a couple of black painted wooden tommy-guns. They got on stage to do their routine and were almost to the point where Steven was supposed to break into a dance. Suddenly, Steven looked down to discover that the whole cast was gathered around the stage. He didn't have a chance to think about what was going on, because at that very moment they all charged up and pulled them off the stage. The first performance of the show was a great success. The service club threw a little party after the show for the cast.

Obviously, there was no longer any question left. Clearly, he must meet this woman. It was clear to him now that it was God's will that they meet. How or why or where, he did not know. He felt he had a mandate, and now Steven would find out why.

You may not have had an opportunity to notice it yet, but Steven does have a talent for getting into difficulty. Thursday was far from being an exception.

Steven reported to truck school. On the third morning, the students practiced driving in reverse with a small trailer attached to the truck. Steven's dad was a truck driver, and Steven thought that he remembered how the big boys did it. He set the hand throttle and climbed out on the running board to look back to guide. He sure did. The truck speed increased, the truck went to the left and the trailer to the right. They moved right along until the trailer hitch put itself against the tail gate. Then, everything stopped. The chief driving instructor, a big sergeant, walked slowly to where the tongue meets the truck, he looked very closely at the damage, and then went around to the other side and looked. Then he backed off from the mess and folded his arms across his chest. He looked down at the ground, and then he shouted, "Where in the hell is the idiot that made this mess?"

Steven came forth and slowly held his hand up. He needn't have, as everyone there knew who did it.

"OK girl, go get in that jeep over there, you are restricted to quarters until you are told otherwise. Do you understand?"

"Yes sir," he said. His heart sinking fast because of the weekend he had planned.

"Incidentally, Private! If you as much as touch the wheel of that jeep, you're court-martialed!"

Steven's heart sank even lower, as he just knew he'd never get out of jail. At least there was no show that night, but there was on Friday night. He remained in his barracks. The next morning he had an escort to breakfast. His heart sank even lower. He remained in his room until ten o'clock. At that time he was escorted to the captain. He was shaking like a leaf.

The captain said, "I understand you had a little problem yesterday. As a matter fact, quite a little problem, wouldn't you say? Here, take a look at this." He handed Steven a piece of paper.

Steven read, "One trailer tongue $1,941.51." Steven gulped

and beads of sweat broke out on his forehead.

The captain continued, "They wanted to court-martial you and give you a statement of charges for the damage. Fortunately for you, the legal office has already decided that a soldier in training can't be held responsible for any damage that he causes as a result of that training."

The captain smiled, ran his fingers through his hair, and said, "Why do I get all the screw ups? You're dismissed. Incidentally, I think you're too nice a guy to be in trouble all the time."

"Yes sir," Steven replied. He broke off a snappy salute, and then exited at an incredible rate of speed. The captain with both elbows on his desk placed his head between his hands and just shook it.

A couple of the members of the cast asked to ride with him to the city in the afternoon. Steven knew only one thing. Tomorrow he would be in the city. That seemed to be enough to know at this point. They got into the car at noon and headed for Capital City. Steven parked the car and went up the hill to church for confession. He dearly needed to be right with the Lord at this moment.

Steven went down and picked up Peggy, and they went to the dance, after he took her home, he parked the "hotel" in its usual spot and with what seemed like a forever effort, finally fell asleep. His friend the sun awakened him again.

He crawled out from under his blanket, put on his tie and jacket, and went to mass. He received communion, and after he returned to his car. He was a little upset that he had not seen her yet. Perhaps he had really been foolish to start again looking for her, but no, he could not turn back now. He went to eat lunch, after which he took in a movie.

When the movie let out, the time was just right, and he went to the Y for the dance. She wasn't there. He stayed till the end of the dance. When it was over, one of the girls invited him up to the parlor. He accepted the invitation, and followed her to the elevator. They rode up, and as Steven got out and entered the room, she was seated at a table across the room. She was dressed in a plaid shirt, a pair of jeans, and a pair of penny loafers. He managed to stay relaxed, even though his heart was tearing his chest apart. He went over by the ping-pong table and sat down, watching the TV across the room.

After a while, she got up with another one of the girls and started to play ping-pong. Steven looked over his shoulder and offered to play the winner. After a short time the other girl won, so he played her and won. His heart pounded as the young lady rose and picked up the paddle.

"My, my name is Steven Mack," he said.

"I'm Cynthia, Cynthia Little," she replied. "Are you in the Army?" she inquired.

"I'm in the Army at Fort Patton"

"My fiance is stationed at Camp Concord, and I don't get to see him very much."

At that point the ping-pong game was over. There was music in the background and he asked her to dance. He was ecstatic being so close to her. After several dances with little talk they sat down. She took out a cigarette at this point, and so did he.

They lit up and as they did she said, "I went to see my mother last weekend"

Steven said, "Oh, you mean in Farmertown?"

"Why, yes . . . but how did you know? Are you the soldier my house mother told me about?"

"Yes, I'd like to talk to you, is that . . ."

"Let's go out on the balcony." She rose without hesitation and led Steven out through some double doors to the balcony.

The moon light, in its fullness, was their only light. They were alone.

Steven spoke. "I need to tell you exactly what has happened to me from Easter Sunday morning until I ate supper in the Farmertown bus depot." Steven told the story to Cynthia. She was absolutely amazed, and told him a bit about Howard, her boyfriend. They had entered in to a quiet, comfortable conversation, even though they had just met. They were alone on the balcony. She could sense his honesty, and she felt a warmth for her from him that she had not often felt from people,

She volunteered, "My physical problems stem from birth defects. When I was born, my right leg was much shorter than my left. My right arm was also under developed and my hand, as you can see, was but a palm. They did not bring me to my mother for two days. When I finally arrived at her side she went into a state of depression. After a number of weeks of this depression, Mama came to the conclusion that God gave me to her for a reason. After that, she buckled down to the job of preparing me for the real world. I guess my poor old daddy was in worse shape. I have never walked a normal, unaided step in my life. The first time I walked was with the aid of a pileon at the age of one, with great joy. By the time I was five, they had worked out the device for me that they expected I would wear throughout my life. It was a brace attached to a ten inch platform on the bottom of my shoe.

"Fortunately, I was just grateful to be able to walk for the first few years. Thank God for my mother. If it hadn't been for her determination that her daughter was going to have every possible opportunity to lead a normal life, I just wouldn't be here talking to you right now. When I was old enough for the first grade, my mother went to the school . . .

"I wish to speak to Miss Armstrong."

"But, you spoke to her yesterday, Mrs. Little" the attendance clerk said.

"That's all right, I want to see the principal, now!"

"But, Mrs. Little, she has already given you her last word."

"But, I haven't given her mine, now go tell her that I am here."

"No, I will not!"

At this point Blanche Little charged right passed the clerk and entered the principal's office.

"Well, Mrs. Little, what are you doing here in my office?"

"I'm about to talk to you, Miss Armstrong, that's what!"

"The conversation was finished yesterday, so, get out!"

"It is not finished," said Mrs. Little. "My daughter must go to this school."

"She may not, she is handicapped, and you must take her to the school for children with orthopedic handicaps. That's the rule here. We cannot take care of her here."

"That is precisely my point. She is an exceptionally bright girl. Regardless of the way she may appear to you, she is perfectly capable of taking care of herself. On top of that, her older brother is here, and he can handle any problem which might arise."

"That's all well and good, Mrs. Little, but I won't take the responsibility."

"You listen! My daughter is going to lead a normal life, and I don't think that you would want to interfere with that, would you? She's got to be with normal kids if she is to feel herself normal and she must also learn to deal with people who have not been so unfortunate. Now, do you understand or do I have to come back tomorrow and explain it again?"

"I'll see what I can do. I will take it up with the district tomorrow, I hope that the appeal will be successful."

"Mama won! Wherever there was a fight, Mama was right there. She was going to see to it that I got every possible opportunity." Cynthia stopped talking for a few moments and lit up a cigarette.

Steven told Cynthia about a few of his things, like the show, his dancing, and his interest in acting, which led him to consider attending the Pasadena Playhouse. He told about being on the high school wrestling team, and about being business manager of the high school newspaper. He talked about a few other things, but what he was hearing from Cynthia was so incredible that he didn't want her to stop. He just wished that the evening would never end.

"My parents were really geniuses. They dared the impossible with me, and because of them, I have been able to handle most every situation in which I have found myself. They decided that I should take music lessons. I liked the idea. I decided I would like to take violin lessons." She lifted her right hand, and almost chuckled as she said, "They got a violin instructor to come out. He was with me about ten minutes and excused himself asking to go to the bathroom. After a half hour, Mama knocked on the door. Hearing no answer, she entered, to find that he had left by the bathroom window. You know, we never did see him again. That was a bit foolish to call him in the first place.

"I had no fingers on this hand when I was born. They operated on it nineteen times. As you can see, they cut into my palm twice to give me three fingers. Only the first two fingers are of use. Now that has been very painful for me physically, but it has been a godsend for me because I am able to use my hand now for so many things. I really don't know how I'd get by if it hadn't been done. We got a piano teacher. I learned to use my new fingers by learning the piano classics. He stayed with me for about ten years. I've become pretty proficient at the piano, but the piano lessons were not the bottom line. They got me a voice teacher, and I was trained up to having an operatic singing voice. You wouldn't believe it to hear me speak, but I have a very high soprano voice. We went out and I gave my first professional singing concert, at a national convention at the age of four. It's really not the easiest thing to do for anyone, but for me, it just terrified me at first. Now, it has built a confidence within me that is not easily shaken and it has contributed to what I have become. You know, I was on the girls' softball team in high school." She paused, and we lit another cigarette.

She continued, "When I was thirteen years old, I skipped school one afternoon and caught a bus to College Square Hospital. I asked to see the orthopedic surgeon who had done the operations on this hand. He graciously called me into his office and offered me a chair. I sat for a long time. He could see that I was troubled, and finally he said, 'Cynthia, what can I do for you?'

"After a little hesitation, I said, 'Dr. Fredrick, I don't like the way I look. I can't wear my clothes properly. I just need to be more normal. Please, can you help me.'

"'Cynthia, what do you have in mind for me to do for you?'

"Tears began to roll down my cheeks and I said, 'I don't know, there must be something . . .'

The doctor reassured Cynthia, "You are very serious, aren't you, my dear. We have climbed a few hills together in the past, haven't we?"

"Yes, and if there is just one more, perhaps we could climb it. Do you have an idea?"

"Cynthia, the one thing we can do is get rid of that right leg. It just isn't doing you any good. If we were to amputate it right about there," He pointed to a spot just below her right knee, "then you would be able to wear a below-the-knee prosthesis which would, for all intents and purposes, make you very normal in appearance. Here, slip your brace off, and set it aside for a moment."

The doctor went over to his closet as Cynthia asked, "Wouldn't that be painful?"

" Yes, it would be at first, and over the years it probably would not cause any more pain than your hand has, but Cynthia, you are used to pain by now. It is obvious by your coming here what kind of pain you fear most. I don't imagine that you would be away from your normal activities for more than three months." He returned from his closet with an artificial limb for a below-the-knee amputee. "You could probably wear one like this. Stand up," he said, he slipped the prosthesis under her skirt and over her knee so she could get a good idea of how she would look.

"I looked in the mirror and could see myself in a full ruffled skirt and a pair of three inch heels! I smiled, didn't say a word, put my brace back on, left the office, and headed home. As I neared the bus stop, tears of utter joy and excitement flowed down my cheeks. I told Mama about it and she grinned, and never let on that she had known of the possibility for years. This relieved her of the need to come to me in the near future with this information. Six months later . . .

"I came into the kitchen to Mama, from school, tears were flowing down my face. It was the middle of May, and school was soon to be out. I told Mama about a boy that sat down to talk to me asked me if I would like to go to the dance with him.

I sat there thinking, knowing I had no business going to a dance, but it would be nice. As I thought that, he turned and walked away laughing. 'Oh, Mama!' I cried . . ."

Blanche put her arms around Cynthia and tried to soothe her, as Cynthia buried her head in her mother's bosom. Then Cynthia moved back from her mother, and looked her straight in the eye, and said, "Mama, its time!"

"Yes, my darling, it is. I'll talk to your father."

"Mama, it's my life, he's got to agree."

"He will, darling, he will . . ."

"I had one week of summer vacation. On that Sunday night, I entered University Hospital. The surgeon came in and talked with me a little that evening, as the surgery was planned for the next morning. He said that he thought that if everything went well, I could go back to school in September. I smiled, thinking of the looks on the kids' faces when I showed up. He pulled my leg out from under the sheets and showed me the exact spot at which he planned to take it. It was just below the knee, in a perfect spot for the best mobility. I had been praying for a long time that I wouldn't be frightened. You know what, Steven, I wasn't! I was at home in a week. Daddy came to the hospital with his big arms and carried me to the car.

"I stayed in bed for almost another week. It was getting very tiresome for me, so I talked Mama into letting me try the crutches. The next day I was up and dressed. At the end of a month we went to the prosthesis center so they could begin building and fitting me with a new leg. I'll tell you, that was a rough time. It is a difficult process at best, and I thought it would never be right. At long, long last I had my first leg.

"On the first day of school, Mama was late in driving me to school, on purpose, I think. When we arrived, Mama let me out of the car and went on home. I got a little nervous as I opened the classroom door so very slowly. As soon as my classmates saw me, their eyes got as big as saucers. Then suddenly they all jumped out of their seats and ran over and surrounded me. We hugged, and danced and jumped for joy."

Steven smiled as he felt her every word. He was both sorrowful and joyous at the same time. Finally, he took her by the hand and said, "Cynthia, you are the most beautiful person I have ever met."

She didn't say a word. She just grinned, and inside she knew that he was telling the truth.

He asked her, "When will you marry?"

"I don't know," she answered, "but if he doesn't go overseas, it will be soon."

"And if he does go overseas?"

"I don't want to think about it. Perhaps I would break the engagement."

"But, why would you do that?"

"Well, as you have noticed, I have just now spread my wings. I am, for the first time in my life, living free. If he were to go overseas, it would be too constraining for me, I believe. I feel like Jonathan Livingston Seagull, I need to have a time of my own to reach for the stars. That's why I'm not in college right now. I need this first. My brother is in college. He will be a lawyer like Daddy. He is two years older than I. The one thing that I regret, Steven, is that I won't be able to wear high heels for the wedding."

"What's to prevent you from doing that?" he asked.

"An artificial leg is stiff in the ankle, so that a leg can be worn with only one heel height, In order to wear high heels I would need a new leg, and that just isn't possible for Howard and I right now."

Steven looked over at the window and noticed that the lights of the parlor were out.

She said, "Oh, it's late. I think we must go. I have thoroughly enjoyed the evening. I feel that we know each other."

As they entered the parlor, she reached over and flipped on the lights. She went over to the piano and played softly for Steven for about fifteen minutes.

When she finished playing, he suggested that they go for a snack. She said that was a great idea, and she rushed upstairs to change into a skirt. They walked over to the restaurant, had a snack, and returned to the Y. They stopped at the front door, and gazed at each other for a moment, then he spoke.

"Cynthia, this is an evening that will live with me forever."

"I can tell . . . I can feel just how much you mean that, Steven. It means more to me than you will know, also."

Then Steven said, "I must tell you something . . ."

She put her finger to his lips and placed the side of her little hand to her lips and said, "Please, don't say it. I already know. This is all there can be. You can't know how sorry I am that we can't really become acquainted." She turned her cheek up to him.

"Good night, Cynthia," he said as he kissed her lightly on the cheek.

He watched her as she entered the Y. He turned, ever so slowly, and crossed the street to his car. He got in, turned the key, and headed into the night.

Cynthia rode the elevator to the third floor parlor. She found the piano in the dark and started to play, ever so quietly. She closed her eyes and let her mind wander. She had no peace just now. She knew that even though she had just met him, he was in earnest. He seemed to be honest, and he was filled with understanding. She loved Howard so very much. He meant more to her than anything. She stopped playing for a few moments. Just for this moment, she was hurting for Steven. She had the feeling that it was not a small matter for him. Then she gave the piano one last bang, and went to her room.

She had undressed and was about to get into bed when suddenly there was a bright flash of lightning. A large silhouette of her shown on the wall, and she saw herself—WHOLE! A summer rain storm ensued. She went to bed. She thought of Howard and Steven, but sleep did not come for a very long time. As she lie awake, she thought also of who she was becoming. She was very happy that she was engaged, and soon to be married to Howard.

By the time Steven got out of town the rain was pouring down. It was difficult for him to see at best, but on top of everything else, the left windshield wiper was broken. He pulled the car off the road, took out the new pack of Pall Malls he had just bought at the cafe, and started to think about what had just happened to him. What? Yes, what had happened to him. His body was shot through with rapture. The adrenaline was pumping through his veins at a rate much faster than they were intended to handle.

He was light headed and giddy. If he thought he had cared for her before . . . well, there was just no comparison. As he thought, he got out of the car and into the rain. As he did, he just burst into song. "When you walk through a storm, Hold your head up high." etc. etc. "You'll never walk alone."

He had been looking to find out about this girl who seemed so unfortunate, and he found, instead, the most interesting and exciting person he had ever met in his life. He felt the power of this person, and also the power of a love that was now etched on his brain for all time.

Oh! If he could spend a lifetime with her. But . . . she was engaged!

But, how could it be that Steven had just met her, and she belonged to another.

"Oh God! Where was the justice in that? Must I accept this, Lord, or can I rise up to do battle for what I would have for myself? But, what of Howard? Must he necessarily be a good man? Perhaps he is a wolf in sheep's clothes or a derelict. Perhaps his daddy has lots of money, and he won't have to work. Oh! Hell! Why has this happened to me. Why this continuing veil of tears which has followed me throughout my life. What can I do? Perhaps I could, somehow, get the money to buy her the leg she wants for her wedding. It is but little consolation, but perhaps, for her, joy!"

When Steven arrived at the base, he went to bed, but he was so tense that he did not sleep. When he got to the service club on Monday, he tacked a three-by-five card on the bulletin board, putting the "Black Hotel" up for sale.

That evening Howard called Cynthia. Howard said that his

mother had called and was still blowing steam about the wedding, and children. He said that there was really no way to stop her.

"Have you heard from her any more?"

"No, I haven't, Howard, but I do wish she would get off the subject because it really makes me nervous."

"I know, honey. We'll make it through. You know what, I had one of those sweats again, only this time it was very, very heavy. I can't imagine what is happening with me."

Cynthia thought to herself, could it be connected in some way to Steven? She didn't know how that could be, but the dates matched the times that Steven was around. She said, "Oh, Howard, don't worry. There is nothing to it. It's most likely that it comes from these hot spells we are having."

"Yeah, I guess that you're right."

"Have you forgotten, honey, that as soon as the orders come, we can plan the wedding."

"You're right, my love. Well, sweetheart, I've got to go. I love you so, my sweet. Pleasant dreams, and good night."

She replied, "Good night, my dear, with all my love."

On Wednesday night they gave another performance of *Kiss me Kate* at the Service club. After the performance, Mike, the piano player came over to talk to Steven.

"Steven, I heard about your wanting to sell your car, is that true?"

"Yes, I need the money right now."

"It seems very sudden that you need money. Are you in some kind of trouble?"

"No, I'm not"

"May I ask why you need the money."

"Well, it's a kind of a secret."

"Do you need a lot of money?" asked Mike. "I could lend you some if you want me to."

"No, I really couldn't accept it. I think it would be about six hundred dollars."

"Won't you at least tell me what you need it for?"

"It's a little hard for me to talk about, but I really feel I can trust you. I feel like I need to talk to someone."

Steven told Mike about Cynthia, including the fact that she was engaged and he was in love with her. Then he said, " I want to by her an artificial leg with which she can wear high heels."

"Don't sell your car. We may be able to come up with a better solution. Will you be going to Capital City this Saturday?"

"Yes, I'd planned to," Steven said.

Mike was taking a card out of his wallet as he spoke. "Here, come to this address Saturday around seven, or call."

Steven was puzzled, but he trusted Mike, and he really knew what kind of guy he was just from being around him at the rehearsals.

That weekend Steven arrived in Capital City about five o'clock. He parked in the Y parking lot, went into the Y, and sat in the waiting area of the lobby, looking out the window. He picked up a newspaper and held it high, so no one could see who was sitting there. Sure enough, as luck would have it, Cynthia and a friend passed through the lobby and out the front door. Steven waited ten or fifteen minutes and he was pretty sure that they were going to the restaurant. He walked over to the restaurant, and as he walked in, they were coming out.

"Why, hello, there," Steven said, as surprised as he could sound. "How nice to see you again. Did you have a nice dinner?"

"Why, yes we did," Cynthia replied, as Steven joined them on the walk back to the Y. "Steven, this is my roommate Carolyn, and, Carolyn, this is Steven, from Fort Patton."

When they arrived back at the Y, Cynthia took Steven back up to the parlor. She sat down at the piano and played. She didn't say anything. She just played. Steven so enjoyed hearing her play and everything about her turned to inspiration for him. He had even bought some simple sheet music, and had started to try to learn to play. Actually, he could read music a little, and with simple music he was able to play a few things. Steven thought that there could be no greater satisfaction than reaching someone and helping them to be more like Cynthia. He had no idea how he might accomplish this. He began to have the conviction that there was really nothing impossible for Cynthia, and, perhaps, not even for him. Cynthia finished playing, got up from the bench, and came and sat next to him.

"Steven, this is it! I can't see you again. It just isn't possible. We must not meet anymore. I'm sure you understand this don't you? I know that this isn't a joke for you and I'm not ready to laugh either. I am asking you not to come back for both our sakes."

"I understand, and I'll do as you asked. If I say thank you for all you have done for me, perhaps, you won't understand, but I will always know for what. I can do no less than wish you a wonderful life forever." Steven looked at her one more time, and left the room.

Steven called the Harris residence and inquired about Mike. The lady who answered the phone said that Mike would be there soon, and that she would like Steven to come out, as soon as possible.

Steven drove out to the Harris house, and when he got there Mike, Jamie, and Mr. and Mrs. Harris were there to greet him. After greets were exchanged, Mike, Jamie, and Steven went over to the edge of the grass and sat.

Mike said, "Steven, you couldn't raise half of the money you would need to buy that leg. Your car isn't worth even two hundred dollars."

Jamie chimed in. "We, three, are all entertainers, and we have a lot more entertainers in the show back at the base. The Harris kids also do some entertaining. They also have knowledge of the ins and outs of Capital City. With their knowledge of the city, they should be able to arrange a place for it, and do all of the advance work for us. With any luck, we should be able to raise the money," said Mike. "We like your desire to help this girl."

"Wow!" Steven said. "That is marvelous! I can't believe that you would really go to such an effort."

From that point on the Harris' took over the matters that would need to be taken care of in Capital City. Steven, Mike, and Jamie were in charge of recruiting the talent out of the show.

What really went on at the Harris', during the weeks ahead, was a wonderful gathering of young adults, spending time together and having great friendships with the loving and caring of Ma and Pa Harris. It was a wonderful Christian home. The boys stayed at the Harris' every weekend. The gang put on little shows, they went to movies, they went to events at the Harris' church, and on and on. They dated different girls. It's hard to describe. It's just what happened for about three months.

The next Wednesday, Cynthia received a phone call from Howard, as she usually did, only Howard didn't sound like his usual self.

"Cynthia, I've got my orders, honey." Cynthia heard in his voice that it was not good news.

"Well, tell me, Howard, where are you going?"

"KOREA!"

Cynthia's heart stopped, and then pounded. She couldn't speak. The tears poured down her cheeks, but she made an effort to keep her tears from Howard. "Oh, Howard, what will we do? I want you so, why did they do this to you?"

"I don't know, either, half of the unit got orders for other places in the states, but not me."

"How soon are you leaving?"

"Three weeks. I'll be coming home on Friday night."

"Finally, they let you go. Oh, I'll be so glad to see you in freedom and away from there."

"I guess we can plan our wedding now."

"Yes, I guess we can," Cynthia said softly, even though she really wasn't certain about it right now. "Howard, honey, don't worry, things are going to be all right. I love you so, and I want us to be happy."

"I know, dear. I know you've got lots of planning to do, so I had better start getting ready to get out of here. Give my love to your mother. Perhaps we can go out to the ranch while I'm home. Good-bye with a kiss, my love." He hung up after he said, "Talk to you tomorrow, honey (a little smack over the telephone). Good night, my love."

Cynthia hung up the receiver, and she was drained. She searched a nickel out of her purse and called her father.

"Hello, Daddy."

To Red, his Cynthia was his crippled child, that is the way Red saw things. He missed seeing much of who she had become. He couldn't see how much of himself was in her. Nevertheless, Red loved his daughter more than anything else in the world.

"Hello, honey. How are you? How is Howard doing at camp Concord?"

"Oh, he's just fine Daddy. He's coming home this weekend. Could you meet me for lunch tomorrow, Daddy?"

"Well I'm supposed to go to a bar lun—"

"Daddy, it's important!"

"Sure, honey, I'll pick you up in front of the store at noon, see you then."

"Thank you, Daddy. Good-bye." Cynthia, hung up the phone.

She climbed the hill to St. Luke's. It was nearly dark when she entered. She picked a pew almost in the center of the church and knelt. Kneeling was both difficult and painful for her, but she had disciplined herself to it before she was baptized a Catholic. Cynthia avoided favoritism because of her handicap, even if it were such a small thing as not sitting while others knelt. Cynthia took her rosary out and wrapped it in her hand, but she did not pray it. She said three Hail Marys, and an Our Father, then she prayed to the Heavenly Father. "Heavenly Father, how is it that with all else that you have let me suffer, now this? I praise you, Lord, and love you, Lord, but is there never enough? Lord, you know that I love Howard. How could you have given him to me only to take him away? You know that because he is a private I can't be with him over there, and even if I could, what kind of life would it be? You have given me every opportunity to grow and flourish. I cannot thank you enough. I present you a full and mature person, how can you press this on me. Please, Heavenly Father, don't let him go. But, if he must go, I ask you to please tell me what I am to do.

Shall I marry him and be hamstrung even more than I am in my need to make my way in all the worlds of endeavor? Would you have me single and free? Perhaps it is that you see our children. Is it possible that you don't see Howard for me? Oh God, help me sort this out in accordance with your wishes. God, preserve me from erring in trying to understand."

Cynthia wept deeply for what seemed to her hours. Then, she thought, please Heavenly Father! She blessed herself and left the pew.

Cynthia met her father at precisely noon and they drove to the country club to which he belonged. It was quite nearby. Red opened with, "Well, my Cindy Lou, you sounded somewhat distraught on the telephone last night. Were you?"

"Yes, Daddy, I was, and I am. Howard is going to Korea, and you know that a private cannot take a wife over there with him."

"So, you marry him and wait here for him."

"Yes, Daddy, that's all well and good for you to say, but it isn't at all now like it was during World War II with millions of women married at home trying to get by on very little money till their men returned home. These families parted by a war don't exist anymore. I have already found that my handicap causes me enough discrimination without having to be a deserted Army bride on top of that. I love Howard, very much, Daddy, and I am ready to marry him tomorrow, but if our marriage would cause us a long separation, I think that perhaps I had better wait and see what happens when he returns. I just don't know. I met another boy by the name of Steven, who came to the Y to meet me."

"What are you talking about, darling? You have two boyfriends, after all of these years of not having any boyfriends at all?"

"Oh! No, Daddy. It's nothing like that. He was just so taken with me that I almost regret that I am not two people. I never met anyone like him. He seemed to be inspired by me. I could feel his frustration when I told him that I was about to marry. Oh, Daddy, I love Howard so very much, but I am really confused. Do you think I should give up my own independence and wait for him?"

"Honey, I just don't know. Of course, if you were to get married, you could go to school while he was away. That would give you a good start toward your goals, wouldn't it? You know I wanted you to go to college right after you got out of high school. I understood some of your needs at that time, I'm not so sure I do now. You're just going to have to decide for yourself. I can't really help you with the decision. I'll help you all I can, but I just don't know the answer."

By this time they had returned to the department store, and Cynthia returned to work with a very heavy heart. She had no more than gotten back on the switchboard when a familiar voice came over the phone.

"Hello, Cynthia. This is Gloria. Darling, how are you?" she said. "Isn't it terrible that poor Howard is going to Korea? That will make it very difficult for you, don't you think?"

"Think? Mrs. Walters, what the hell do you care what I think? I'm sorry, but I'm very busy right now," and with that she unplugged Gloria.

Steven had a three o'clock appointment with Mike to go over his part of the "Brush up your Shakespeare" number for the show. It was the final show, and it was to be a command performance for the commanding general of the post. He got in his jeep and went over to the club. He met for about half hour with Mike.

"Steven, Jamie and I have been released from our school and will be returning to our regular bases. Jamie's shipping orders and mine put us on leave as of Friday. The Harris' are planning a party for us this weekend at that park over near Pine Creek. Because it was such short notice, they asked me to tell you, so that we could all be there together."

"Oh, great! I'll be glad to help send you guys off. It's been such great fun these past weeks. I only wish that this little group of ours could go on forever."

When Steven came out of the service club, to his horror, his jeep was surrounded by MPs. As he came out, they immediately asked him if he was Steven Mack. He admitted that he was, and they arrested him for taking a vehicle without proper authority. Steven had done it again. They took him back to the company in the jeep and turned him over to the company commander. After a wait of two hours, he was beginning to worry about that night's performance, because it was getting late. He was called into the captain's office.

"You just don't give up. One scrape after another. For the time being, you're under house arrest. However, due to the fact that the general is a slight bit more important than you—wouldn't you agree?—I'm going to allow you to do this last performance. You will, however, be escorted by two guards, who will have concealed weapons and will remain inconspicuous as long as you behave yourself. Do you understand? You've just been too much trouble since you've been in this unit. At the end of the show, your private escorts will return you here, and you will remain in the barracks until I release you. Is that clear?"

"Yes, sir!"

"Now get out, and don't you dare give these men any trouble."

"Yes, sir."

Steven had a good deal to worry about when he arrived at the service club. It appeared as if he wouldn't be going anywhere for a long while, let alone to the outing for Mike and Jamie. That night the cast gave a stunning performance. The General was very pleased with the show. Steven got through his performance, even though he was just about a nervous wreck. What was the captain going to do to with him?

The next morning his two companions were still with him, but at about ten o'clock, the two guards, who were now armed with carbines, left. Hell, Steven had no plans to go anywhere anyway. At eleven o'clock, the captain summoned Steven.

"So, you're an expert field wireman, are you, Private Mack""

"I beg your pardon, sir. I don't know anything about wire, sir."

"Oh, yes you do. It just happens that they need troops with the MOS of field wireman. Thank God, they don't need drivers!

I don't think I could do that to them, but wireman, I have no sense of guilt about that."

"Sir?"

"Here are your orders, sending you to report to Camp 'I shall never see a tree' Kilmer New Jersey for assignment in Europe. Your delay en route and leave will start tomorrow. You will be paid and checked out of the unit a two o'clock this afternoon. If seen in the area after 2:01, I'm giving orders to shoot your ass. Is that clear? I suggest you stay in the barracks until then. And . . . whatever you do, don't go near the motor pool. I am considering posting guards. Good-bye, Private, and uh good . . . er luck."

That afternoon he received his pay and was checked out of the unit. As soon as he was free of the unit, he went over to see Mike to tell him that he had also been transferred. He told Mike that he was going ahead up to the Harris', and would see him there.

Steven was, in a way glad, that he was leaving Missouri. Thoughts of Cynthia were still with him. She was always on his mind, and he either didn't want to shake her or he couldn't. The truth is, that it was a bit of both. Steven got into his car and drove it through the main gate for the last time. He pointed it for the city of his first love.

Steven was glad in a way to be going home. He had dearly loved his father, who had been dangerously ill with an ulcer for some time. Steven and his stepmother had been at war for years. They just did not get along. Even though his dad wanted to help him through college, he decided to join the Army, and allow his dad and stepmother peace and quiet without kids, which she claimed caused all the problems in the family. However, it most assuredly didn't solve anything.

He would always want to see Cynthia, but now it would be impossible. She would be here, and he would be in Europe. How could such a brief, and less than tragic encounter in love, be so important?

As the "Black Hotel" approached within five miles of Farmertown, the electrical system on the car gave out. Steven hadn't had time to sell it before leaving Missouri. The truth was that it wasn't worth anything anyway. He surely couldn't get it fixed. He just picked up his duffel bag and hitched a ride the rest of the way to the city. Thus ended the "Black Hotel".

Thursday night Steven stayed with the Harris'. They were surprised to find that Steven also had orders. They were no more surprised than Steven. By seven that evening, all three of the boys had arrived and were greeting each other.

Suddenly, Mike said, "What can we do about the show, Steven? We're all leaving, and the plans are pretty well advanced. What are we going to do?"

"Right now, I have no idea. I guess we will have to forget about it. I appreciate the effort everyone has made on Cynthia's behalf, but without our being here, the show can't go on," Steven said.

"We darn well gave it a try. We have to hand it to Jane and Harold, they put a lot of work into the effort. We sure should get the whole Harris family some sort of a gift," Jamie suggested.

Steven suggested, "Why don't we all chip in some money and go shopping in town when we get back from camping?"

"That's a good idea, Steven," said Mark.

Thus ended the quest for the leg. Steven was disappointed, but he knew that there was nothing more to be done.

At the Y, Cynthia was still considering what she should do. She had not much time to decide and she had done everything she could to make a fair and reasonable decision. She loved Howard and wanted to be his wife so much. She needed some semblance of independence and acceptance from the society that knew how to make her life rough. She did not know what to think of Steven. She did not like to see him hurting. She was relieved that he had the good sense to stay away as she had asked.

Then she thought, "My Lord and my God, I put my trust in you, and want only to serve you. I believe that it is your will that I marry Howard. This I will do, in the love of you and Howard, my Lord."

The alarm went off at seven. Cynthia slipped out of bed, and hopped into the shower. Howard was going to arrive at the bus station in less than an hour, and she wanted to be ready for him. She was so very excited about his coming home at last. Cynthia dressed in her favorite outfit and raced around the corner to the station.

The bus was coming into the station as she arrived. Soon the doors of the bus station opened, and Howard charged into the waiting room. Just as he came through the doors, his mother was coming off the street and running toward him. Howard had spotted Cynthia, and saw nothing else. He dropped the duffel bag and threw his arms around her. They kissed passionately. He held her so close and with such tenderness, that she thought that she would lose control.

Finally she said, "Howard, I want to . . ."

"Wait . . . me first. We're going to California, sweetheart, to the great state of California, my love."

Great tears of happiness poured down her cheeks, she could hardly contain her delight. This moment was the happiest she had ever lived. She grasped him tightly around the waist and they embraced warmly. They could feel their heart beats in rhythm. Cynthia was in ecstasy as she pressed closer.

"Thank you, Lord, that this time it came out just right," she thought. Then Howard whispered something in Cynthia's ear.

"No! Howard, not with your mother standing there!" Cynthia pointed over to her left.

Howard looked over to see his mother standing there for the first time. He put his arms around his mother and Cynthia as they left the bus station.

In a few days, they crossed to the Pacific Ocean and Camp Roberts, where they were married by an Army chaplain.

When they had returned from the camp out, Steven was the first scheduled to leave. Mike and Jamie rode, along with the rest of the gang as they drove him out to Air Force field so he could catch an Air Force Hop to California. This was the last time that the boys would be together, ever. They said their fond good-byes and left. Steven's greatest desire right then was

to call Cynthia, but he knew that would be of no value to either
of them. After a wait of two hours he got a flight to California,
and home. The plane was in the air for ten minutes when the
announcement came to fasten their seat belts, as they returned
to the air field. Steven had gotten away, and now, suddenly he
was back. He could not resist, he must talk to her one last time.
He picked up the phone and dialed. Someone answered.

"Hello, Cynthia?"

"No," the voice answered. "Cynthia, is gone. I'm sorry."
She hung up.

Steven hung up the phone, not having any idea what the
party on the other end had really meant, and walked slowly
back to his seat.

Soon, Steven was once again on a plane headed for
California. As he flew over the Red River and the Grand Canyon,
Steven thought of his first trip out of California. It was a tour of
the national parks in the Southwestern United States. They
went as far east as Carlsbad Caverns and El Paso. He was very
lucky to have been on that trip.

Earlier that summer, just before the Fourth of July, he had
gone with a friend of his to another kid's house. They all sold
newspapers at the time. While they were in the driveway, The
kid lit a piece of fireworks, and threw it down Steven's back.
He charged out the driveway and bolted across the street.
Steven's back was literally on fire. Fortunately, there were no
cars on the street. As he reached the other side of the street,
someone yelled, "Roll! Lay down and roll!"

He threw himself on the grass and rolled. Thank God that
someone yelled, as he would not have thought to do it himself.
That person's quick thinking, whoever he was, kept his injuries
down, and it is even possible that he saved his life. Somebody
put him in a car, and rushed him to the doctor. Steven had a
large third degree burn, three inches in diameter, on his back.
The doctor cleaned up the wound, and shot him so full of
medicine that he was sick from it. They wrapped him with such
a thick padding of bandages that he looked like Quasimodo
when he left the office. He went into the waiting room and laid

on a couch. A nurse came down and gave him a shot for pain, and in a bit he was able to get up and go home.

Steven was in the Boy Scouts at the time, and although he had only been in less than a year, he was a second class. This was at the beginning of summer, and they were organizing a fifteen day trip around the Southwestern United States. When they found that they didn't have enough scouts to make up the tour, they lowered the requirements to allow second classes to take part in the tour. His dad asked the doctor if it was all right for Steven to go. The doctor told Steven's father that the burn was not healing, and there was proud flesh in the wound. He also said that if it didn't heal, they would have to do a skin graft. That decision could be made after the trip.

Two days before the trip, Steven went into the office and they cut the proud flesh off his back. He went on the trip, but the medication they put on him made him stink so that no one wanted anything to do with him. What happened to him at this time was minor compared to what Cynthia went through. The purpose of the story will become clear presently.

Steven's plane had now reached California, and they were soon to land. After landing, Steven took his duffel bag and hitchhiked to the Central Valley of California, where his Father's home was. He, fortunately, caught a ride straight through, and he catnapped along the route.

Steven once again turned his thoughts to his accident, which in overall terms was really of little significance now. Immediately after returning from the trip, he went to the hospital for skin graft, as the burn was never going to heal by itself. His father remarried that summer, giving Steven joy in the thought, however temporary, that at last he would have a mother to live with. That became a shattered dream, also. His family moved to Central Valley, and he entered junior high school for the first time. Steven never really understood why he had such a difficult time making friends. The immediate problem was that he was not to be allowed to take gym with the other students until his back was properly healed. He remained in the gym by himself and shot baskets.

He could hardly contain the excitement of it all. The car in which he was riding stopped on the highway just north of the park. He hitched another ride and the driver was nice enough to take him home.

Steven remained home for about a week and was becoming quite on edge. He wondered about Cynthia, he wondered if he would ever see her again, he wondered at the power of the feelings of love that ran rampant in him. She was constantly on his mind. He wondered about the woman who really couldn't exist, but she did! He decided to leave for New York immediately and visit there for a week, as he had always wanted to do. He had an ambition for the theater as a profession at this time and had not quite come to the point of being willing to give it up it yet. But, the idea of becoming a physical therapist was really beginning to interest him. If he could move but one person on the road toward living a full life, that would, after all, make his life very successful life. Just one!

He had a nice visit with his father, whom he feared he would never see again. Steven told his dad all about Cynthia. He told him about the strange circumstances of their meeting. He told him how very deeply he loved her. His dad told him that the most important consideration in choosing a mate is to be sure to know what kind of person they are. Finally, Dad said, "From what you have told me, she may very well be a very good woman. It's too bad that you didn't get a chance to find out."

His father and stepmother took him to the bus station. One reason Steven chose the bus was because it was the cheapest way, and he could save some of his travel pay. He would also be able to stop and see the Harris'. Perhaps he might even see Cynthia.

When Steven arrived at the Capital City bus depot, the Harris' were waiting for him. Mom Harris put her arm around him in a loving greeting. They whisked him to their house. On the way home, they joyful talked of Mike and his fiance, who were soon to marry. Everyone talked about how fortunate Mike was to get such a lovely woman. With all the happy talk, Steven was not ready to bring up Cynthia.

When they had finally arrived at the house, Mom Harris got something from the desk and handed it to him. It was a newspaper clipping, with Cynthia's graduation picture on it. Cynthia and Howard had been married at Camp Roberts the previous week. Steven went into the bathroom, locked the door, closed the toilet seat, and sat on it. He cried in a frustration that he could hardly bare. Finally, he washed his face and rejoined the group.

He just couldn't stand to be in Capital City any longer. He was distressed, even though he knew that things could only work out this way. He caught the bus for New York the next day. For Steven this had become a very stressful thing to happen. As a matter of fact, it was the most stressful time of his life.

Steven remembered the first time he had experienced the stress, a boyish love. Steven was in the eleventh grade. During this particular year, he had a study hall, which was very unusual for him. He never had much studying to do there. Strangely, he started thinking about a little friend who lived near him in Grape Arbor, a town near central coast of California, when he was in kindergarten. Her name was Mary White and they used to play together. One day she went to town with an older girl. They were walking on the train overpass when she slipped and fell. Her face was badly cut along her jaw. It was not a disfiguring scar to any extent. She was in the hospital for a few days, and Steven recalled that he sent Mary a purse at the hospital.

This was in the middle of the year, mind you. A few days later, a girl walked into Steven's eleventh grade drama class, registered, and sat across from him. Steven looked at her in total disbelief, he leaned over to her and said, "Aren't you Mary White, from Grape Arbor?"

She was startled and said, "I'll talk to you, after class!"

After class Mary and Steven met in the hall and gazed at each other in disbelief. Then Mary spoke, "You're Steven Mack, aren't you?" she asked.

"Yes, how wonderful to meet you again like this?"

"You know I can't get over the fact that, for some strange reason, you were heavily on my mind, just last week," Steven said.

"I've been married and divorced, and I work evenings at Sammy's restaurant. I live with my mother next door. See you later, I've really got to run," she said and gave him a little peck on the cheek as she left.

He went home that night and was wild with excitement. He really was not at all successful with girls when he was in school, and when he saw Mary in this very unusual way, he was overwhelmed. He had difficulty sleeping for a couple of nights. As it turned out, Mary, having been married and having had quite a hard life, was obviously too mature for Steven. This wasn't easily accepted by Steven, but he did accept it.

The really ironic part of all of this was that Mary had injured a finger a short time back, and after their meeting had to have the first joint of her middle finger removed. This was very painful to Steven. Steven cried over it when he found out about it. The combination of these two things drove into some very great distress. This was the first time that he had felt such discomforting feelings. Although his feelings were almost unbearable, he just did not understand why he was so completely upset.

After several days, Steven arrived in New York. He spent a week there. With the interest he had in drama, he decided to investigate the various drama schools in New York and he attended five plays. Steven now noticed something else. For the first time, he watched every where he went, for a woman with one leg. It was the only answer he knew for his failure to win Cynthia. The woman that he had no concept could exist had so taken him that it seemed impossible there could be another woman to compare with her in any way. Steven had to try. If she existed, Steven had to try to find her.

Steven met a Catholic girl of his age by the name of Maria at a USO dance. The evening they met she took him to Greenwich Village, to a place called Tony Pastures.

Steven reported into Camp Kilmer to await orders to embark. Wait, hell! In two weeks at Kilmer Steven he had three KPs and two guard duties. On Wednesday evening of the last week, Steven had a date with Maria. He was in a hurry, so he didn't pick up his pass. He had on civilian clothes, but was also wearing a full length Army issue coat, which unfortunately had a buckle missing. Maria and Steven had a wonderful time seeing *Tea and Sympathy* with Joan Fontaine. They talked about various books, including *The Caine Mutiny*. Maria had said that Steven was much like Ensign Kieffer. Steven escorted Maria home, and then went to the port authority to catch a bus home. With his broken belt buckle hanging out. Steven soon found he had company. Two MP's were nice enough to escort him home, and they even provided his company commander at Kilmer with a discrepancy report for his being out without a pass and wearing the uniform improperly. Steven never heard anything about the discrepancies before leaving the United States.

Steven had but one more detail to pull. It was guard duty, and Steven sometimes enjoyed it because it was an excellent time to think. Guard duty usually consisted of two)shifts from six in the evening. Each post was covered by three guards. Each guard walked two hours then had four off. Steven's first shift was at midnight. Steven thought about the fact that he was leaving America for a long time. He wondered about what was ahead.

Cynthia was gone. Where would he ever find another person to inspire him as she had? The feelings he had about her at first were changed by her into the greatest love he had ever known. The piece was gone. How would he ever find it? He had really been alone most of he life. He could have given Cynthia so much. He just knew that she would have given a great deal to him. He loved her, body and soul. Oh, he loved her body to be sure, but it is her very being and mind that he could not escape. My God, what could he do? He couldn't possibly go about seeking a mate based on Cynthia's sheer guts and energy, or her courage, or her bravery. How could he find them? The only hope would be to seek first a woman who was physically like Cynthia, and hope that they might be also be like her in mind and spirit. Perhaps an acceptable substitute? Oh, God! Was that possible?

The next day he picked up his duffel bags, climbed on a bus, and went to the boat. Steven boarded the ship of duty and, thus, started his quest to regain the missing piece.

A time for every thing, yes!
A time to laugh, and a time to weep
A time to search . . .

There were short periods when Steven thought he had found the piece. It was not so. There were short periods when he thought he had found the piece once more, but as it turned out this was not to be. There is no desire, though, to take anything from Herta, for as you shall see, she was, indeed, in her very own way, a very remarkable woman.

Well then here is . . .

Section Two:
Herta

As Steven boarded the USS *Buntner* for his free passage to Europe, his thoughts turned ever more toward Cynthia. The little he knew of her, was of great comfort to him. Even though it might never be, he still could draw pleasure from thoughts of being intimate with her. There were so many other things about her that he liked to ponder. She was a great inspiration to him.

Steven's bunk was on the middle aisle. Even though it was in the middle of everything, Steven was not annoyed by it. When he wasn't pulling KP, he spent time writing letters. He wrote a letter to his father. He tried to write a letter to Cynthia's mother as he knew that he couldn't write to Cynthia. It was a thirty-five page letter in pencil. When Steven had finished, it needed so much editing that he went out on deck of the ship, tore it into small pieces and threw it overboard.

The trip went well until the sixth day. Steven had been learning to play double deck pinochle. He never found out how they chose him to sit in on their game, but he would always be grateful to them for it. Pinochle had a great significance and impact on him later on in life. Steven would say that, indeed, it was very important. He stayed up very late every night playing.

On the sixth morning of the trip, when he had KP, he didn't make the four A.M. call. As a matter of fact, he didn't get to the mess hall until 6:30. Steven was sure he was in big trouble. Well, he was in trouble all right, but not as bad as he had thought. He had to work through until midnight. Now, that wouldn't have been so bad, except for the fact that Steven had been on the run ever since he left Missouri. He made it through the shift, but he was worn out.

One evening he had a chance to go up and watch a movie.

He didn't take a jacket with him and it turned out to be a bit cold. There was a rather large fellow about Steven's age sitting beside him. The fellow just reached out and put his arm and jacket around him. Steven thought that was one of the kindest things he had experienced.

The next day, they passed the White Cliffs of Dover. After being at sea for two weeks, they docked. It was a treat to see land after seeing nothing but ocean for so long. The huge ship was sitting peacefully at dock. The port was Bremerhaven, and soon after day break, the gangway was put in place and what seemed like an endless stream of soldiers, their duffel bags over their shoulders, filed orderly off the ship. The single line continued to waiting trains, which would seemingly meander through Germany to finally stop at the reassignment depot at Zwibruchen (Two Bridges).

Steven managed his duffel bag and finally came to rest in his seat on the train. The trains were much like the ones you see in European movies, with a single aisle on one side and private compartments for six to eight people with glass door enclosures. Unfortunately, as Steven discovered, none of the glass in the trains was safety glass.

He was glad to at last be on land again. He was looking forward to his new post. He felt that he needed a change

The train moved along quietly. The country was very green. Steven found that it was a beautiful country, although there was much rubble from the bombings. There were many bombed out buildings, including a church in Hamburg which was completely flattened. But, what Steven really perceived was that wherever there was rubble the Germans were busily cleaning it up and preparing to rebuild. The sight was awesome, and Steven found it very encouraging. He saw these people persevere after having the hell torn out of their country.

Steven was on the train for about twenty-four hours. There were times when Steven wasn't convinced that he was going anywhere. Every few hours the train would come to a stop. Then, after a little bit, it would start moving in the opposite direction. Steven decided some years later that this must have been some switching maneuver, because they never returned to the same place.

It was January 1945 in Eastern Germany. The air raid sirens had started to blare just fifteen minutes before. Herta still had not heard the familiar, devastatingly frightening sound of the roar of planes overhead. Herta, only eleven years old, her ten year old brother Franz, her six year old brother Wolfgang, and her mother were in an air raid shelter just outside of Dresden. There was room for only twenty people in the shelter. It was the nearest one to their house and it was full of neighbors. There was but one dim light dangling from the top of the bunker. Wolf was crying, for he knew what was coming, as well as any of the adults in the bunker. Herta was also frightened, but prided herself on being grown-up enough not to show it. Suddenly, there was a roar in the distance. The shelter, where a moment ago there was the buzz of busy talk, suddenly grew silent.

In the distance could be heard the explosion of bombs as the planes came closer and closer to their bunker. Wolf's cries became louder and more hysterical as the noises of the planes neared. Herta took him and laid him on the floor of the bunker against the dirt wall, and placed her body over his to protect him from harm. Mutti, as the children called their mother, protected Franz in a similar manner. Soon the planes came closer and closer until the very bunker in which they were shook from the concussion of the bombs. The small light over head swung to and fro. Small drivels of dirt fell from the ceiling. There was a great explosion, so close that the entire bunker was lit up like daylight. Then the sounds were suddenly less menacing and the drone of the aircraft became fainter and fainter until the all clear siren could be heard.

Mrs. Hausen gathered up her children and watched them as they climbed the steep ladder out of the bunker. It was noon and the sun shone bright, except for the clouds of smoke from the fires that had been started by the bombings. When they looked toward their house they found that the house next to it had been destroyed, and even now was on fire. When Frau

Hausen saw the house in flames she lost her self-control. She threw her fist in the air and cried, "Kreutz Donner Vhetter!" ("Why must they destroy us! We have done nothing to deserve this.") Her anger was not for herself, but rather for her children. They, all four, stood at their home staring at the house across the lot. They were just numb. Then, without welcome, the air raid sirens began to blare once more . . .

It was night time now, and the train had just left the Old Bahnhof at Heidelberg. It was a dirty old place, and the trains pulled into the station and then backed out. Steven got up out of his coach, and went out into the aisle to have a smoke and stretch. There was a rather large soldier out there who had a nasty, bragging disposition. Steven really didn't like him, and he strongly suspected, even though he didn't remember for sure, that it was he, Steven, who had started the fight. He had also lost the fight. This was how Steven had discovered that German trains do not have safety glass. His larger opponent easily pushed him partially through the train's outer glass. That was the end of the fight. Steven received a small but deep cut on his back. Of course, the MPs came by to make a report. Steven hadn't even found his new home in Germany and he was already in hot water again.

Steven returned to his seat. The wound, while deep, was also very small. He found himself in a completely new world. He had no idea what it was going to be like, but he really wasn't concerned. He was sure that he, if no one else on that train, had fallen upon exciting times. His thoughts turned to someone who had been a close friend . . .

Steven had moved to Central Valley during the fifth grade. His father had left him with one of his fellow truck drivers to live with while he was going to school. As soon as school was out, Steven's father sent him to a summer camp near a lake in the mountains for a month. Steven had a wonderful time, except for some home sickness for his family, which came about because the relationship between his father and mother was at an end. There were times when no one came to see him on the weekend, and he cried for hours.

When Steven returned home from the camp. He went back to Grape Arbor to live with his grandmother for a while. He had a friend who lived up on the hill, above the railroad tracks near him. That summer, Richard and Steven were almost inseparable. Richard was very handy with tools, and he built a soap box derby race car while Steven very carefully watched. As long as Steven just watched, everything went along fine, but Richard didn't want Steven to build his own. As a matter of fact, Richard was using a pair of wheels that belonged to Steven. The relationship became so close that Richard begged Steven to go to his school the next fall. Steven liked the idea and agreed that he would.

On the first day of school, Steven reported to Richard's school, which by now he had his heart set on attending. The principal of the school told him that he could not attend Richard's school and that he must return to his original school. Steven was broken hearted and cried bitterly as he rode his bicycle over to the other school.

The kids in the other school were delighted to see Steven, as he had been away in Central Valley for about a year. The day passed as a normal day, and Steven enjoyed being with his old classmates, but his thoughts were still on his buddy and the other school. The kids in his old school begged him to forget about going to the other school.

Late in the afternoon, the principal of the school came into the classroom and announced that the classroom was over crowded, and that they would like to send some students to the other school, if there were any who would like to go. Steven, knowing that this was a put up job, thought for a few moments, then volunteered to go.

This was possibly Steven's biggest mistake in his young life. Steven's emotionalism along with constantly being with Richard wore thin quickly. Once the friendship cooled, there really weren't many people in the class who Steven knew well. On top of this situation, Steven became ill around Christmas and had to have his appendix removed . . .

It must have been shortly after midnight when the train finally arrived in Zweibruchen. The soldiers picked up their duffel bags and filed off the train, all accept Steven, that is. He was instructed to wait until he had an escort. Steven thought, oh nuts! He was really in a jam now. He was certain they were sending the guards for him. There was nothing he could do.

Presently, to Steven's great relief, two medical corps men came to him. One of them shouldered his duffel bag, and the other ushered him past long lines of soldiers to the infirmary. A doctor examined Steven's back and put a couple of stitches in it. Other than being rather tired from the past month and a half activities, Steven felt great. They ushered him to a private room in the infirmary and Steven bedded down for a good night's sleep, never suspecting that no one else who got off the train that night went to bed at all. That's what comes from screwing up. Steven slept soundly. He was really worn out.

He slept so deeply that his breakfast, neatly placed by his bed, was cold by the time they were finally able to wake him. He had a leisurely breakfast, and afterward put on his travel uniform in preparation for being shipped to his new duty station. The orderly at the hospital showed him where he must report to pick up his orders, and there was never a word spoken in regard to any disciplinary measures.

At noon, Steven boarded the train and headed for his new duty station in Karlsruhe, Germany. It would be a very short trip, so Steven decided to settle back and read *The Stars and Stripes*, the U.S. military newspaper.

Herta was but sixteen years old when she glided carefully on her crutches through the open back door of the shop of Henrich Braun, Certified Prosthetist, in Heidelberg. She had been told some months before that Herr Braun was the finest limb maker there was. Herr Braun came from a family of limb makers. His father had owned the business before him, and his father's father before him. There was one thing about Herr Braun, and that was that he was fully dedicated to providing his customers with the best limbs that could be built. He took each customer's individual problems to his own heart, and he always delivered to those for whom he worked. After meeting him for the first time, Herta decided to take his recommendations to heart.

She had only lost her leg a little over a year ago, and right then she was very uncomfortable and in a bitter mood, having to get around without a leg. It was very difficult for her, both physically and emotionally. She was much like a duck out of water. Her future seemed bleak indeed to her at this time. Soon, an older gentleman appeared in the hallway. He was a short man with a pudgy stomach. He was not fat, mind you, but pudgy. He had a round face with sparkling eyes. He was in his late forties, and he held the stub of an unlit cigar in the side of his mouth. You knew, the moment you saw him, this man was alive.

When he saw her, he gave her a great smile, and said, "Aw Herta, perhaps you took my advise. Yes!"

"Yes, Herr Braun, I was just released from the hospital, after having the revision you recommended. What misery this is, and for what?"

"Patience, little one. If you please. Herta, go into that booth over there and remove your skirts. Let me know when you are comfortable."

After a few moments, Herta said. "All right, Herr Braun, I am ready."

Herr Braun entered the booth carrying his small stool, which he placed before her and sat. Herta's left leg had been amputated above the knee. Herr Braun looked closely at her stump, pushed on it in a few strategic spots, then looked Herta in the eye with his broad smile.

"You would like me to make you a leg, ja? The doctor you went to did a very good job for you. I congratulate him. Now we will make you a proper leg. I wish you could see the potential as I do."

"Why, yes, Herr Braun I must do better than I have been. I would be very pleased for you to build me a leg."

"We will take a cast of your stump, and the other necessary measurements, and then, if you will please come back in two weeks, we will be able to start fittings."

After the preliminary measurements were made, Herta took her crutches in hand, and with a perceivable bounce in her movement exited Herr Braun's, soon to be familiar, back door. Herr Braun thought to himself, "I have seen so many—some from the war, some from accidents, and some pitifully from, soon to be, fatal disease. There have been beautiful women, and cute little children, as well as the bad and the ugly." He had seen them all. This one! In this one there was something special, there was in evidence a quality that was very hard to put your finger on. He was looking forward to fitting this girl. She most assuredly one day would be a very beautiful lady. She must have a leg that would have some hope of being worthy of her. She must have all the knowledge of wearing it as her talent will allow her.

Herta walked along the narrow street, away from the shop, and toward the Haüpt Strässe, where she could board the street car that ran along the side of the narrow street. As she was about to get on the street car, she felt the fine touch of a woman's hand on hers. As Herta turned, she saw the hardened but pleasant face of a woman about ten years older than she. She had auburn hair and was dressed in a smart two-piece business suit. She had on a pair of low cut light brown shoes, and Herta hadn't noticed it yet, but Inge had an ace bandage wrapped around her left ankle.

"Excuse me," the woman said, "but perhaps you would like to talk to me?"

"Bitte [I beg your pardon]? But why?"

"My name is Inge, and I am wearing a prosthesis."

"Oh? Why yes, I might like to speak with you!" replied Herta.

Herta pulled back from the street car, and she and Inge started up the street. Herta noticed for the first time that Inge indeed was wearing a limb, and she walked with a great deal of difficulty.

Herta and Inge sat over tea for at least two hours. During that time Herta asked Inge why she wore an ace bandage around the ankle of her prosthetic leg. Inge explained that she thought that fewer people would notice that a prosthesis was the cause of her limp. In that time Herta was able to find the answers to many questions that she had no one to ask. They talked about how difficult it was to go out in public, on crutches, with only one leg coming out of her skirt. It bordered on embarrassment. Herta said that she almost felt a sense of guilt when in public. Many people stared at her, and that made her feel uneasy. She knew that they meant no harm, and she was sure each one of them felt pain for her; nevertheless, she still felt uneasy. Inge could offer Herta no comfort in this matter. The only thing was to get off the crutches. This meeting was a wonder. Inge had also been to Herr Braun to get her legs. The two women hit on a friendship which never ended . . .

Steven stared out the window, watching the gardeners in their little garden patches along the side of the road. They couldn't have measured more than twenty-by-sixty. Each one had its own tool shack right in the middle of the patch. At one point, Steven had mistakenly believed that the gardeners actually lived in the tool shacks. As it turned out, the Germans were not quite that bad off.

Steven found an article in the newspaper about a tryout for a show in Frankfurt to be held the next evening. Steven thought that it would be nice to try out, being that he was still interested in acting.

The signs along the track began to read "Karlsruhe" and he new that he soon would be at the end of the trip. Steven shouldered his duffel bag and headed for the train exit. As he moved through the Bahnhof he heard the words "Actung, Actung." It was a word Steven was familiar with from many war pictures. It had always been delivered harshly. It was now being delivered almost melodically, and its sound was intriguing and very refreshing to Steven. As he stood on the boarding ramp, the top of the Bahnhöf was possibly a hundred feet above his head. It was shaped in a huge arch. There were sections of glass to provide cover. Many of the glass plates were missing. Steven guessed that they had been broken out during the bombings, and had not yet been replaced.

Steven walked through the station until he reached the side walk. When he got there, he was met by a tall, lean corporal who inquired, "Are you Private Steven Mack?"

"Yes, that's me," said Steven, as he handed his sealed records to the outstretched hand of the waiting corporal. The corporal also offered Steven his hand to shake and announced, for the first time, at least to Steven's ears, "Welcome to Neuröit Kaserne, Karlsruhe, Germany. My name is Corporal Ted James."

"Quite a welcome, Corporal, I must say. Where are we located?"

"We're about ten kilometers north of here. Come get in, it's just a short ride from here. The largest weapon we have is a 1.5 rocket launcher. We have no canons. We are strictly for observation. Now, what did you say your MOS was?"

"I'm a wireman," replied Steven.

"Oh—ah—yes," was the corporal's retort.

The rest of the ride was without event.

Upon arriving at the Kaserne, Steven was given a bed and was issued blankets and sheets. He met a few of the guys that he would be living with. He had finally decided that he would try to see the captain in the morning about going to Frankfurt for the tryouts.

At 0730, before morning mess was complete, Captain Casey entered his orderly room. He was fiftyish, and had been in the service for thirty-one years. He was a bit stooped and had the butt of a cigar crammed in the side of his mouth. He was nearly bald and what little hair he had was gray and stood straight up on his head. When you first saw him, the immediate reaction was that he was a harassed man. It might well be that his wife was the guilty culprit, or perhaps it was a combination of her and the Army. At any rate, Captain Casey was definitely not in a good mood. He entered his office, unlocked his desk drawer, and took out a fifth of Scotch and a small cup. He poured himself a drink and downed it. He placed the bottle and cup back in the drawer before he picked up the new personnel record lying on his desk. He read the name—Private Steven Mack. He broke the seal and proceeded to look through the record. The MOS of wireman caught his eye almost immediately. He said to himself, "Oh shit, that's one of those MOSs they use when they want to get rid of someone. You bet your ass, he doesn't know a piece of wire from a hole in the ground. Oh! Well look at this, will you! The first man in Fort Ord history to contract poison oak while being confined to the base. Ha, ha, now let me not be hasty, but the private sounds like a screw-up to me. Let's see, Fort Patton, failed to pull first cook shift due to drunkenness . . ."

The captain shouted to the outer office, "Corporal, where in the hell is my coffee. Oh, never mind. I have it." Having discovered his coffee, he poured just a bit of a taste into it from his bottle.

"He was transferred and then he wrecked a jeep. No charge. Then he bent the trailer hitch in deuce and a half school. Hasty hell, he's a screw-up. How do I get all the eight balls?" At this the captain's blood pressure was beginning to rise steadily. He lit the half inch of the cigar he had been chewing, turned to the next page, and continued to read.

"He stole a jeep to go to the service club. I'd have had him court-marshaled and in jail by now. Oh, but now I see, that's how he became an expert wireman. They decided to shove him off on me. Isn't that damn sweet of them? I have half a mind to send the bastard back. That would damn well show 'em and save me a lot of trouble to boot. That happened only three months ago." The Captain then said, "Well that's understandable with these yo—. Wait, there's another page here. This is from Camp Kilmer N.J. Oh yes, out of uniform in a New York bus station, and without a pass no less. Where is this little SOB?"

With this, the company clerk charged into the captain's office asking, "What is it, sir? What is it?"

"Just hold on a second. There's just one more page to this damn thing, Sometimes they say nice things on the last page, isn't that so, Corporal?" The Captain was nodding his head up and down trying to get some agreement.

He read for the clerk. "He picked a fight with a six-footer

on the train, that was yesterday, and was put through the glass. Oh, we've got to do better than this. He'll ruin my damn reputation. We don't want that, now do we, clerk. Corporal, bring me this Steven Mack, not that I want to see him, just bring him here."

"Sir, he's out in the orderly room. He has asked to see you."

The captain furled his brow in puzzlement. You might even call it a look of astonishment. He chomped on his cigar.

"All right, get me a fresh cup of coffee, and," with a deep sigh, "show the SOB in!"

Steven entered with what was the closest thing he could manage to a smile as the captain said, "Remain at attention!" The captain got up from his desk and began slowly circling Steven. He inspected every aspect of him.

He continued, "Your a phenomenon, boy, a genuine by-damn phenomenon. I don't believe it. How in the hell have you survived, boy? I've always thought it was the survival of the fittest. Well, now wait, perhaps that is the answer, perhaps you really are very fit. Now if it be possible, we may be fortunate enough to find out for what? You wanted to see me on your first day in my company. Oh, no, don't tell me. I know you thought that if you came right over, we might negotiate a lighter sentence. Yes?"

"Sir?"

"Perhaps, you thought I might give you the court-martial myself, if there is one."

"I beg your pardon, sir?"

"Tell me, Private, how does one manage to screw up so fast and so often as you and still remain on the loose? How long do you have left in your enlistment?"

"Sir, two years."

"Well, that's just too damn bad. With this list of failures— example, going through a train window—really, you probably won't leave the base until you go home. You might not even make it home! You know I'm supposed to get all the smart guys in this company, so give me a believable explanation . . . No, no on second thought don't," said the captain, who was beginning to pull on some of his very last strands of hair. "Now you wanted to see me about something, Private?"

"Why uh, I mean, I, a well I do . . . really think tha—?"

"Out with it, damn it, Private, what is your problem?"

"Well sir, I'm an actor of sorts."

At this, the captain's eyes grew large in disbelief.

"There is a tryout for a play tonight in Frankfurt, and I'd like to have permission to go, sir."

The Captain was sipping his coffee at this point and spit a bit of it across his desk, as he almost swallowed his cigar.

"You, what?"

"I said . . ." said Steven.

"Never mind, I heard you. Corporal, come in here! Now, Private, you go to your quarters, and stay there until I send for you, even if it's two years from now! Do you understand?"

"Yes, sir!"

"Now move out, and keep in mind, if you disappear from there, I'll hunt you down with some unrehabilitated German shepherds. Is that quite clear to you?"

"Yes, SIR!" replied Steven, his eyes relaying a sense of total bewilderment at this point.

After Steven left, the captain took the bottle and cup out of the drawer, poured himself a stiff one, and shook for several minutes. He sat at his desk and just thought. He had a damn good group of men and they didn't give much cause for the need of punishment. He sure didn't need a rotten apple now. Finally, he broke out in a maniacal smile and called out, "Corporal!"

"Yes, sir!"

"Type up an overnight pass for Private Mack," said the captain, almost laughing.

"But, sir!"

"Do as I say, Corporal. You see, Corporal, if we let him go, there is a forty percent chance that he'll get lost, and a forty percent chance that he'll wind up in the Frankfurt brig, and a forty percent that he'll be killed in a train accident, and even a forty percent chance that he'll be thrown through a train window.

Don't you see? Letting him go right now is our only chance! If you add up the chances, it comes to a 160 percent chance of getting rid of him." Evidence of madness was creeping over his face as he spoke. He pulled the bottle out and took a swig.

By noon, Steven was dressed in his civilian clothes and headed for the Karlsruhe Bahnhöf. There was in each Bahnhöf a special place for the military to buy their tickets. The tickets were half price, and were a portion of the reparations the Germans were paying the Americans.

When Steven reached the front of the line, he told the clerk that he wanted a round trip ticket to Frankfurt.

The ticket agent inquired, "Would you like first, second, or third class?"

Steven thought for a moment, then asked, "Which one gets there first?"

"Why, they all get there at the same time," said the clerk, with a puzzled look. "It is a matter of accommodations on the train."

"Well, in that case third class will be just fine," he replied.

Steven got on the train and settled back in his seat, where he almost fell into dreamy sleep.

Herta, using a pair of forearm crutches, entered Herr Braun's shop. It was just two weeks since she had last seen him, and she was quite excited about seeing her new leg. The moment he saw her in the shop, Herr Braun showed her to a booth and went to get her leg. Herta was aghast when she saw it, and wondered what she would ever do with a thing like that. He told Herta how to put it on, and for the rest of the day they worked at getting the leg properly adjusted. That is a difficult, if not, at times, an impossible task. Finally Herta was satisfied. She quickly discovered that with a proper length skirt, she might look quite nice. She had forgotten, for an instant, about how nice Inge had looked.

Herr Braun said, "Please, fraulein, walk across here again." Herr Braun also thought to himself that Herta had many problems to deal with concerning proper walking with that leg.

Part of the problem was that she didn't have any experience at this time. Part of it, such as the toe up caused by the stiff ankle and the floating leg action coming from the uncontrolled knee, was common to most amputees. He thought, this child is so robust, and so physically well coordinated, that it could be that with some intensive training she could do quite marvelously. He had never trained one of his clients intensively before, but this girl could well be worth the trouble.

"Herta, could you come to the shop every morning for a time?"

"For how long, Herr Braun? "

"As long as it takes!"

"As long as what takes?"

"Oh, forgive me, I'm ahead of myself. I would like to give you intensive gait training. A fraulein as lovely as you should not have to walk around as one who is tipsy. If you will come, we will learn to walk beautifully!" Herr Braun had never seen anyone who could walk like that with an above the knee amputation, but he was not going to let Herta know that fact.

"That sounds good to me, so, then we can start tomorrow. May I wear my leg home today, Herr Braun?"

"Why, yes, of course." He said with a broad grin. "Until tomorrow at nine o'clock."

Herta met Inge for tea on the Haüpt Strässe, and told her of Herr Braun's plan.

The train was just pulling out of the Heidelberg Bahnhöf, ready to start the last half of the trip. Steven's thoughts turned once again to his time at school during the sixth grade . . .

Richard had wetted Steven's appetite for building a soapbox racer. He also had a strong desire to see soapbox racing for kids in Grape Arbor. Steven tried unsuccessfully to get soapbox racing started. He did, however, start to build his own car behind his house at night. He worked from the plans that a well know auto manufacturer had put out. The car that he was putting together was somewhat more sophisticated than the one Richard had built. After getting about half of it finished, he came home one evening from the movies and discovered that someone had taken a hammer to the car and destroyed it. Steven and Richard talked about it and decided that the mean kid that lived at the end of the block must have done it. Steven started to build the car again, only this time he locked it in the garage when he was finished working on it. Once again, one evening when he returned from the movies, he found that someone had torn the lock off the garage door, and destroyed the car. At this point Richard gave up on building a car. Many months later, Steven realized that the mean kid down the block didn't have any reason to destroy the car. Indeed, he might not have even known that there was a car being built. It was obvious that it was his friend Richard, out of apparent jealousy, who had destroyed the car . . .

The train was pulling into the Frankfurt Bahnhöf. The service club to which Steven must go was one and a half blocks down the street, after coming straight out of the Bahnhöf. Steven wandered around in the middle of Frankfurt and got himself a bite to eat. At seven o'clock, Steven entered the service club to join the auditions. To his dismay, and perhaps even his embarrassment at being there, he discovered that what he had read about in *The Stars and Stripes* was actually a local club tryout, and was not a general call to the Army in central Germany. Steven remained for the tryouts, and afterward he went to a nearby cave bar with the group and had a couple of drinks. Steven remained over night and caught a train back to Karlsruhe the next morning. His pass was good until noon. Steven felt, for some reason, that he didn't want to be late. Steven boarded his train and found a comfortable seat.

It was two days after VE-Day on the outskirts of Dresden, and never so much joy had ever been heard coming from Herta's family. Herman, Herta's father had come home. He was an officer policeman in the German Army. It was the first time they had seen him in over a year and a half, even though he had been less than a hundred miles away. He was a huge man, and his favorite, Herta, loved to cuddle up to him. All the children gathered around his chair while he sat and rocked, and they even delighted in just watching him smoke his pipe. Mutti was in heaven as she baked and cooked constantly, even though the variety of available goodies to cook was sometimes in short supply, or completely lacking. The party, or party like, atmosphere went on for two days before Herman finally announced that he had to return to his post briefly, and that he would leave the next day. Everyone gathered around him to wish him well, and at the same time to beg him not to go. Herta especially begged her father not to leave. Finally, the big man gathered up his things and, at about noon, he started off to the east. Herta grabbed at his pants leg and tried to hold him. Finally, she alone followed him out about a hundred yards, sat on the ground and wept. She stayed there for about a half hour until he was finally out of sight. It was the last time anyone ever saw him. He was murdered in Poland.

When Steven returned to his unit he reported to the captain. He told him that the whole thing was a farce and apologized for all the fuss and bother. The captain said that it was quite all right, and that he should report to wire section leader. The only thing Steven couldn't quite understand was Captain Casey's look of gloom when he saw Steven. At any rate, Steven spent the next day and a half getting acquainted with the men, equipment, and the wire section. To this point he had no knowledge of what his work was going to be.

The next day was relatively quiet for Steven. Lord knows he needed it. He hadn't yet caught up on his sleep. He spent most of the day learning how to splice wire and how the crank worked on the take up reels. Apparently, his main job in the field would be to lay and pick up wire. Now that didn't seem to be so complicated. While running behind a three-quarter ton truck, the layer, pulled the wire off spools on the back of the truck.

It did occur to Steven that he might do well to be in good shape before tackling this job. He hadn't been in shape since his last wrestling season in high school. Dancing and singing, at least the way Steven did it wouldn't keep anyone in shape. That evening Steven went down to the enlisted man's club for a couple of beers, after which he went next door to the service club where they were having German girls in from Karlsruhe for a dance. Steven turned in about midnight. The whole battalion was asleep when "Practice Alert!" came over the battalion radio. It was a frequent occurrence, and no reason for alarm, but right then a radio operator noted time 4:05 A.M. and alerted the battalion duty officer that the battalion must move out to the field immediately. Steven woke up when the lights in the barracks came on, and seeing how rapidly everyone around him was getting dressed, he did likewise. When they went outside, the trucks had already been pulled into the area, and Steven was told to get into one of the three-quarter ton trucks. It was still dark when they started to move out. By the time they stopped, the sky was beginning to become light. The order came to lay a telephone line. At first there were three men on the back of the truck. That provided one to pull the wire, one to stake the wire alongside the road, and one to catch his breath inside the truck.

Herta entered the shop once again. This time she had the feeling that Herr Braun had accomplished what he had set out to do. They had been working together for five months. He had instilled in her a belief in her ability, which she felt she was able to stand on. She had a hope that he would say it was finally right. Herta's walk had lately become so good, that she noticed that people did not seem to be aware of any differences between her legs. On this morning Inge was in the shop when Herr Braun asked Herta to slip her shorts on and take one last walk for him in front of the mirror.

"Yes, my dear, that is perfect. I never thought that I would live long enough to see it. But, you have accomplished it. Now, you must keep your mind on it at all times, so that you will never allow your gait to slip away from you. You see, Inge?"

"Yes, Henrich, I also am very proud of her. You have done an amazing job. It is to bad that all amputees can't walk like she does."

They laid wire until six that night, when the exercise was over.
Steven's butt was dragging the ground by then, and he was
ready to head for the barracks. After about a forty-five minute
delay, for what reason he had no idea, the order came to pick
the wire up. One of them would reel it in, another would run
behind the truck and keep it straight, while the other one would
pull the stakes and untie them from the wire. They worked
along until eleven o'clock that night, and they weren't even
near being finished. Steven was in a state of near collapse, and
they finally let him go in to the barracks at four in the morning.
The fact that he had failed to finish the job put him in a bad
light in the wire section. He felt, personally, that now he was an
accomplished wireman, which, after all was said and done,
wasn't anything to be proud of.

Steven really liked to go off by himself in town to explore.
When he got his first regular pass, he walked over to a little
town about a mile away called Old Neuröit. This was his first
real time out of the barracks, and he felt like kicking up his
heels. It was to be his first experience drinking German beer.
As he arrived at the village, he went into each Gasthaus and
drank a glass of draft beer. By the time he had gone through
town, Steven, who couldn't hold his liquor any way, was drunk.
As a matter of fact, he was very drunk. One might wonder how
he got to the barracks in one piece. One might wonder, indeed.
In fact, he didn't quite make it back to the barracks in one piece.
Somewhere along the way he was relieved of his money, and it
is a mystery to this day where the money went. That wasn't the
whole worst of it either.

When Steven woke up he had one hell of a hangover. When
the corporal tried to get him out of bed for roll call he challenged
him to a fight. Well, no fight occurred, but when the wire
sergeant heard what had transpired, he was not exactly
delighted. He wasn't delighted to the tune of a two week
restriction for Steven. Steven figured that the restriction, on
balance, was probably overdue.

After his restriction was over, Steven went, quite often, into

Karlsruhe on pass. Wherever he went, he would always be on the lookout for someone who could replace Cynthia. He never saw anyone! He continued his search. He did meet Isabelle, a girl who had no handicap, through a couple of GIs who joked unkindly about her, and took advantage of her sexually by getting her drunk. Steven dated Isabelle, and they became buddies for the whole time Steven was in Germany. Isabelle had a baby boy, by a GI from Hawaii who had promised to marry her but skipped out instead. Steven found that Isabelle really wanted to live in the States. That didn't cause any problem in their relationship. Steven had told Isabelle about Cynthia, and how he felt about not being married to her. Sometimes Steven and Isabelle would go to mass together. To Steven, Isabelle was a very nice girl, and that was how he treated her.

To be sure, by now Steven was considered the biggest screw up in the outfit. He liked to sleep and would sneak away and take a nap whenever he got a chance. One day the guys were sitting around in the barracks shooting the bull. Steven was sitting on the floor over in the corner of the room kind of dozing off, when the conversation turned to him. He pricked an ear, and pretended to continue to doze.

Someone said, "You know, Steven sleeps more than Tex, the radio operator, and you know how much time they have off. They don't even pull inspection in there sleeping quarters."

Steven thought that sounded like a much better job than chasing a wire truck to lay the wire, just to turn right around and pick it up. All of that time off, wow! The radio operators worked four hour shifts with sixteen hours off between shifts.

Two days later, the chief radio sergeant came by and asked, jokingly Steven thought, if anyone would like to go to radio school. Well, jokingly, Steven raised his hand. The sergeant explained that a man from Head Quarters Battery had already been chosen to go, and would leave a week from Monday.

One morning, a few days later, they were having morning roll call when a hell of a roar came from the direction of the orderly. The captain's voice could be distinctly heard, if nothing else. Steven might have been a little paranoid, because he really thought he heard his name mentioned in the midst of all the four letter words. By the time roll call was over, Steven was a little shook up. If the captain mentioned his name, he couldn't imagine why. He hadn't done any thing wrong since that first drunk.

That very morning Sergeant Rameriz, the sergeant over the radio operators, came looking for Steven. He told him to get packed because on Sunday he was going to Darmstadt to attend radio school. This was a shock and a happy surprise to Steven. From the way it had first sounded, if he did get an opportunity to go to the school it would be at a much later date. Now Steven surmised that the captain was not exactly happy about his going. When he first entered the Army they gave him a battery of tests. One of the tests was a radio Morse Code aptitude test. They gave the codes for four of the letters in the alphabet, and they wanted to know how quickly and how well they could be learned by listening to them through a headset. Steven never gave the test another thought, and had no idea how well he had done. He surmised that after his first mention of the school to the sergeant, he went and pulled Steven's record and discovered that he had a much higher score on the test than the fellow they were sending. They pulled his orders and sent Steven.

He had no control over the situation, he was just lucky. It seemed that the deeper Steven got into the hole, and the more trouble he got into, the better he made out. It was not true that you would call Steven, exactly lucky. If he made it through the thirty-six months of active duty without a court-martial, at the rate he's going, then you might be able to call him extremely lucky.

At four o'clock Sunday afternoon, Frank Smith from Charlie Battery, and Jim Hart of Able Battery, along with Steven, had their duffel bags on the boarding platform, waiting for the train to Darmstadt. When the train finally arrived, they picked the first drawing room. They decided to pass the bags chain style into the compartment. Steven was receiving the bags as they came into the compartment. He threw them up on the seat, as they were passed to him. Unfortunately, the railroad hadn't yet installed safety glass in their trains. At, any rate, Steven managed to throw one of the bags, part way through the window. At least, no one was injured, and the boys shared the forty mark charge the conductor needed for the glass. They settled down for the trip to Darmstadt.

Steven's thoughts once again turned to Cynthia. He wondered how she was doing and truly believed that she was happy. He wondered if his love for her would ever die, or even cool. How could it ever be satisfied now. He stared out the window for a moment . . .

It was just three days after the war's end, and Mrs. Hausen had been informed that she and her children would have to move on. They could only take what they could carry. Their house no longer belonged to them. The Czechs took over everything, including the house which had been in the family for over ninety years. The police inspected the goods they were carrying, and confiscated anything of value that they found. The family decided to strike out for the west, believing that they would get better treatment from the Americans than they would from the Russians. They were on foot when the four of them struck out for Berlin.

These were hard days, with the stench of dead bodies everywhere. Some of the rubble they passed was still smoldering. Food was very hard to come by. Luckily, Mutti was able to hide their cash in a place the police failed to look. She had quite a bit of money, and thus they got by reasonably well. The trip to Berlin took more than three weeks. When they arrived, they were met by Mutti's brother. He told them that the border was closing, and that they must get a train out of Berlin. He had some small connections and finally arranged for their transit on the last train from Berlin, destination Heidelberg . . .

The first morning at school turned out to be a rude awakening. They had roll call before breakfast, and were marched off to the gym to do what is politely called the daily dozen. This is a set of Army exercises, designed to keep its fighting men fit. Steven thought that this was a terrible experience before breakfast. Besides, who in the hell wanted to be fit anyway? The officer in charge of the company to which he was attached believed in preparedness. He believed strongly that it was his duty to be prepared to meet the Russians should they attack across the border. He was convinced that one day they would come. That was exactly what he did. He was a fine officer.

The school's format was unusual. The whole idea behind it was to teach the soldiers International Morse Code. The procedure is fairly simple. The students sat a tables with head sets on and copied code. That was it. As you can imagine, this would be an impossibility for eight hours a day, so they usually copied code for two hours in the morning, and two hours in the afternoon. In order to pass the class you had to reach a speed of thirteen words a minute with a minimum of errors. A sending speed of thirteen words per minute was also required. Classes were an hour between breaks, but long before an hour, concentration would be broken and the soldiers either played games on paper or daydreamed.

When Steven was a small child of about three, he slept very fitfully, and his parents could not keep covers on him at night. They finally wrapped him up like a papoose and pinned him into his blanket. It helped a lot. When Steven was five years old, he was aware that his grandfather had an artificial leg. At that age he used to go into his closet and pretend that he had only one leg, and he didn't know why . . .

This group, of soldiers, was both interesting, and unusual. To begin with, there were no dummies in the group. They were all chosen because they had the possibility of becoming radio operators, which most of them succeeded in becoming. There was one soldier, who showed himself to be the smartest in the group. He showed his intelligence not only in the fact that he learned code rapidly, he had a good deal of general knowledge and acquitted himself well among his fellow soldiers.

On the other hand, there were a bunch from a tank corps in Mannheim, one of them was also near the top of the class. He, however, declared himself the smartest person in class. These tankers, and their friends were true bullies. They would go to town together and push the German civilians off the sidewalks. They were hostile to anyone who was not with them. Steven had never known such people before.

Steven passed his receiving test on the ninth week of the eleven-week school. Sergeant Jones, who was the assistant in the school, happened to meet up with Steven one morning, and the started to talk.

"How do you like the school, Mack?" he asked.

"Oh, its just fine! It is really different, that's for sure."

"How long have you been in the service."

"It's been twenty-one months now."

"You haven't made PFC yet?"

"No, sir!"

"Do you know that if you don't make PFC by the end of nineteen months, you can request a discharge?"

"Yes sir, I know that."

"Why haven't you applied?"

"Well, it's like this. I joined the Army. I didn't want to at the time, but I joined. I hate the Army, I hate it with a passion. There is something in me that doesn't like to lose. I hate to lose, and I believe that I can make a success of it yet before I am discharged."

"Well, all right," Sergeant Jones said. "You are doing quite well in school now. You keep it up, and I'll write you a recommendation when you leave here. In the meantime keep up the good work."

"Thank you, sir."

A few days later Steven went into town one evening. He had a few beers, and then a few more beers. At one o'clock in the morning, Steven was walking down the streetcar tracks singing "When You walk Through a Storm" and tears were rolling down his cheeks. He frequently thought of her; as a matter of fact, it was rare when he didn't think of Cynthia.

The next day, Steven had a hangover. He could hardly hold his head up it was so bad. They were calibrating their radios that afternoon, but Steven could do nothing. Sergeant Jones finally came by, and upon seeing Steven's condition, put him on restriction for two weeks. The restriction lasted almost until the end of school. It also was the end of the sergeant's recommendation.

Steven spent his first December in Germany. On Christmas day it snowed for the first time that year. Steven appreciated it very much, as he had not seen a lot of snow.

While Steven was restricted to the base, he called downtown and asked for a girl he knew to come out and visit him. She said she would be happy to come out and visit. She was handicapped, having had polio. They had a nice time, and they went to see *Rear Window* together. She came out to visit him again over the next few days. The last night, when she went home, he got on the bus with her and escorted her home. They were together for two or three hours. As it turned out, nothing was hurt by his leaving the base without a pass.

Finally, it was graduation day, and everyone received their diplomas. Everyone also received orders to return to their home bases, and headed for the train station. Steven and his group got on the train and settled back for the leisurely trip to Karlsruhe.

On the very same day, Herta stepped carefully off the train in Bremerhaven. She almost tried to run when she spotted her boyfriend on the platform. He stopped her muted charge, put his hands around her waist, and swung her around once, putting her gently down. He topped that off with a gentle, loving kiss. He took her bag as they started out of the station.

Herta was only visiting Han for the weekend, but they were both very excited. Han was leaving for the United States on Monday. He was an aircraft mechanic, and one of the major carriers had offered him an opportunity for additional training. Han was a handsome man to be sure. He was five feet eleven inches with curly black hair and an olive complexion. He and Herta really looked very nice together. They cared for each other quite a lot, even though they had really known each other for a very short time.

Han brought his car to the station and they toured the city

on the way to eat. Herta was hopeful that one day they might be married.

Herta and Han had met six months previously in the market place in the old town square. They were seated quite near the City Hall, just in view of the Heidelberg Castle. When Herta viewed the castle after her accident and observed the destroyed guard tower, it reminded her of her own broken body. In a way, she related herself to the destroyed tower. She reminded herself of how beautiful the castle was and she felt sure that the half destroyed tower contributed more than a little bit to the castle's loveliness. She was very much aware of her own beauty. Han and Herta happened to be sharing the same table while having an ice cream. Herta was already seated at the table when Han arrived. They struck up a conversation. Han told Herta about his work as an aircraft mechanic, and Herta told him about her part-time work for an attorney. When they had finished their ice cream they got up and walked together to the streetcar on the Haüpt Strässe.

By the time this all happened, Herta had become an expert walker, and Han did not notice that she was wearing an artificial leg. She had decided that there was no need to mention it, just yet.

When he left her at the streetcar stop, they agreed to meet on the next morning in front of the post office. He told her that he must return to Bramerhaven the day after tomorrow. They spent a pleasant day together. They even went out to Handshühscheim, where Herta lived, to meet her mother. By the time they reached Herta's house, what with all the climbing on and off streetcars, Han was fully aware that Herta's leg was missing. He had no need to mention it, however. The three of them had lunch together in Handschühsheim.

Herta and Han returned to Heidelberg and went to a small Gasthaus, with a patio in the back, on the Haüpt Strässe, to have an afternoon beer. They talked of many things, especially about seeing one another again, after he returned from the States. They dined together at the Ritter, the most elegant old restaurant in Heidelberg.

Then Han said, "Herta, I cannot say what a wonderful two days I've had with you."

"That's true for me also. I like you very much. I hope that we will see each other often in the future."

He replied, "I would like that, very much. I really don't want to leave you so soon. Will you stay with me tonight?"

Herta hesitated a moment, then said, "I . . . don't know, I mean, don't think I a—"

"What are you trying to say? Don't you want to?"

"Why, I, uh . . ." She didn't know what to say. She wanted to say yes, but she didn't think he knew about her leg. If he didn't, they could be in for a big disappointment she thought.

"Herta, I know that you have an artificial leg. That is not a problem for us."

"Oh," she smiled with a sigh of great relief. "Oh, well, forgive me for not having mentioned it to you sooner. I suppose that it was not quite fair to you. I'm sure that you can understand that it is not my favorite subject of conversation. Yes, I would love to go with you tonight."

That night, after they attended a movie, they went to his room. He put out the lights, knowing that she would feel a little more comfortable.. They undressed in the dark. She slid her leg off and got under the covers, laying her naked body against his.

After spending the weekend in Bremerhaven, Herta saw Han to the boat Monday morning before returning to Heidelberg. She was filled with joy and anticipation of a fine future, as she returned home, even though the subject of marriage had not come up.

As soon as Steven returned to Neuröit Kaserne, he was transferred to the radio operator's sleeping quarters. There was no inspection, no roll call, and generally no wake up time, except to go on shift. There was a shortage of operators, and frequently non-operators also pulled shifts, with a senior operator. There was but one radio operating in the battalion. It was at Battalion Headquarters. Thus, all three of the operators that came back from school worked at the same place. As has been said, when you are scheduled on shift, you work four hours, then you are off for sixteen hours. Sometimes Steven was asked to do additional work in an afternoon, but mostly he could get a pass or do whatever he liked.

One of the reasons there were two men on a shift was because they had to operate a hand crank generator. It had two handles, and the cranker sat on a seat attached to the generator. This was not hard work for the most part, because the messages that were sent were very brief answers to the queries of V corp. headquarters in Darmstadt. One of the important tricks, and it surprised Steven, was that he needed to be able to take one of the cranks off the generator, clip the sending key to his knee, and while turning the crank, send a message. There was a regular message every half hour to verify that all of the stations were in touch with headquarters. This ability was valuable, when one of the operators decided to go to lunch or to the restroom. Steven thought that this was how he learned to pat his head and rub his stomach. It was great duty, and it was nice belonging to such a neat club. Steven was a senior operator, and he enjoyed his work.

Now, you would think that, with a job like this Steven would stay out of trouble. In a manner of speaking, he did. That is, he never got in trouble because of this job. Steven had a couple of problems, however, that could have gotten him in a lot of trouble. First of all, when he worked the midnight to four A.M. shift, he tended to fall asleep. That's not the worst of it. Frequently, when he was to work the four to eight A.M. shift, they couldn't get him out of bed. Be that as it may, he finally became a PFC three months after becoming a radio operator. Steven was proud of finally making PFC. He tried very hard to stay out of trouble. You have to give him credit for that, don't you?

About that time there was a tryout for parts in a musical comedy in Heidelberg. It would involve three months of temporary duty in and around Heidelberg for those not stationed in the area. Steven asked his sergeant for permission to go to Heidelberg for an evening tryout. The sergeant gave his permission, and Steven was off again on the train. Heidelberg now had a proud new train station. Steven reported to Patton Barracks that evening, where the tryouts were being held. The director was an American. He was not a soldier, but he was employed by special services. The show being produced was *Wonderful Town*. Steven told the director, Erich Rome, in the initial meeting that he had experience as a dancer. He was sent to the dance tryout area. The dance director was a tall slim fellow with professional experience. His name was Jerry Stein. He was a superior dancer, and as he proved an excellent choreographer. At the end of the evening, Steven was invited to join the show, and he gave the information necessary, so that the director could make a request to the special services officer, Captain Bradford, for the temporary duty assignment. He was to be with the group for the run of the show, three months. They were going to request that Steven be assigned to start the following Monday. His new station would be in Seconheim, a small village between Heidelberg and Mannheim.

Steven returned to the base and reported to Sergeant Rameriz what had happened. The sergeant, who was very pleased, said that even though he was short on operators, he was hopeful that the captain would let him go. The request from Seconheim reached Captain Casey the next morning.

That next morning, at about ten, the operators were lounging around in their room, along with Sergeant Rameriz. Suddenly they heard a terrible noise from outside somewhere. They went over to the window and listened to the roar. It seemed to be coming from the orderly room or thereabouts. Steven was pretty sure that he knew what it was, but he didn't say a word.

The company clerk came charging out of the orderly room and up the stairs. Steven was looking around the room about that time for a place to hide. It was no use, there was none. As it turned out, it really didn't matter because the clerk was looking for Sergeant Rameriz. The clerk said, "The captain wants to see the sergeant immediately, if not sooner!"

"You wanted to see me, sir," Sergeant Rameriz addressed

the captain.

"No, not really, but what the hell is this thing?" he asked as he handed the request for temporary duty to the sergeant.

"Yes, I'm aware of it," Rameriz said, as he quickly scanned the request. "I'd like to ask that he be allowed to go."

"You what! You recommend him to be let loose again?"

"Well, he did go to school without incident, didn't he?"

"We, were damn well lucky. This guy could break a damn anvil, and you want me to let him loose?"

"Well, sir, he didn't get into any trouble, as far as we know in Darmstadt. We just have never had anyone interested in the entertainment field in our unit before, sir. I think that I can spare him, and I would ask that you let him go and let him take advantage of the opportunity to use his talent."

"He sure as hell has a talent, a talent for getting his ass into trouble. I just don't want the unit getting a bad name from this idiot. On the other hand, if he didn't get in trouble I guess it would be all right. I guess. We might even get lucky and they'd put him in the slammer up there. Maybe you are right after all. All right give the paper back, I'll sign it," he said, with his infamous grin. "He is released to them as of Monday morning. His last shift will be on Friday, and at that time he is on pass. Does that suit you, sergeant?"

"Yes, sir!"

"You're dismissed!"

Salutes were exchanged, and after the sergeant left the office, the captain reached into his drawer and poured himself half a cup. He put his elbows on the desk, and held his head in his hands for the longest time.

The sergeant called Steven outside when he arrived back at the radio operator's room. With a big grin, he announced to Steven that the request had been approved by the captain.

That Saturday night, Steven went out with Isabelle. They had a pleasant evening in a Gasthaus, where they danced and drank the evening away. They went to a park and sat until dawn, then they went to mass in a big Catholic church on the eastern edge of town.

Steven returned to the barracks about ten and gathered his belongings. He said good-bye to the boys and was once more off to the train station. This time it was a jaunt of only an hour.

Inge had gone out to see Herta in Handshüscheim that very afternoon. They sat and sipped wine, as they had a habit of doing on Sunday afternoons. Inge had brought her little son with her this afternoon. The baby was only six months old, and it was Inge's first child. Herta was the godmother to the little tyke. It was on this afternoon that Inge first told Herta that she was having a great deal of trouble in her marriage, and that she did not think she could take much more of it. They talked about where she might stay if she were forced to move. She lived in an upstairs flat now, which was difficult enough for her, without having to consider moving. At any rate it was not yet clear that she would have to move. They talked along until early evening, and finally Inge knew that she had to go home. Herta and Inge walked together the short distance to the streetcar stop.

A German made three and one half ton truck picked Steven up at the Bahnhöf and took him off into the sticks where his new sleeping quarters were. When he got there he checked in with the orderly room of the regular duty troops with which he was to bunk. Having nothing better to do, Steven went over to the Enlisted Men's club for a couple of beers. When he entered, there were a couple of Secenheim frauleins who came over to the club with one of the soldiers stationed at the base. Steven didn't find much of interest happening in the club, so he fell to drinking a little more heavily the usual. It was just enough to make him a bit melancholy and he started thinking of Cynthia. It seemed to him that it would be forever that he would love her, and perhaps he was right. How he wished that things could have been different for them. He understood, but it didn't make him feel any happier. He had been in Germany for a year, and although he had watched carefully he had not even seen a woman that could in any way replace Cynthia, in his heart. Cynthia had taken the piece from him totally, not only by physical attraction, but also, even more, by the internal person that she was. That, Steven could never shake. Steven left the club, found a quiet spot at the edge of the Kaserne, and in the light of a full moon, he sobbed lightly, his heart had still no solace. Steven went up to the barracks and turned in.

The next morning, he reported to the special services office. This proved to be quite an informative day. To begin with, there were to be only two persons in the show, on temporary duty assignment. All of the other men were from nearby bases and, therefore, the two of them would be responsible for all the stage craft work. That really wasn't Steven's cup of tea, but what could he do about it? They received permanent class "A" passes, so that they could come and go as they wished. It was a nice thing, but it was also a necessity. There were nightly rehearsals and stage work during the day at the military hospital auditorium in Heidelberg. The final surprise was that the two of them were to get drivers licenses for German three and one half ton trucks. Steven thought to himself, "Oh, why not. Hell, anyone can drive." So, he went to take the driving tests. There was both a written test and road test. He passed the written test with ease. It consisted mostly road sign recognition and driving rules for military vehicles on the German highway. The road test was administered by a German employee of the American government. He was tough. Steven took the test three times before he finally passed.

At this point, Steven didn't really know what he was going to do in the show. Even though he had only tried out for the dance line, the hope some how lingered that he might be considered for a speaking role in the show. Being that he was on temporary duty to special services for the show, he had no worry about being cut.

On this Monday evening there was a meeting of all of the people who had tried out for the show. The cast met in the lobby of an ancient hotel. It was adjacent to the Old Bahnhöf into which Steven had come when he first came through Germany enroute to Zweibrüchen. The main post office was directly across the street. It was a hot night, and all the windows in the hotel were open. It was between six and six-thirty, and Steven was leaning out the window, waiting for the casting to begin. As he watched outside he suddenly noticed a woman, passing in front of the post office across the way. She was limping. Steven was sure that it was more than a limp. He knew from the walk that she was wearing an artificial leg.

Steven left the window, hurried out of the building and down the stairs. As he ran across the street to the post office building he noticed the time on the street clock. It was precisely six-thirty. He did not get very close to her, as he knew that he must soon return to the lobby. He followed until he saw her board a street car at the Platz, marked Handshüscheim. Steven thought that perhaps at that same time on another evening he might have an opportunity to meet her. He hurried back to the lobby, just in time to hear Mr. Rome announce his name as part of the dance team. That was fine with Steven, he was just glad to be away from Karlsruhe, he was also glad to be doing a show again.

The next morning he went over to the laundry service to turn in his dirty clothes. He was amazed to discover that the laundry policy had changed since he left Neuröit and that it would now take eight working days to get it back. He worked the next few days at the hospital auditorium during the day. They rehearsed evenings in various places around town. On Thursday, they rehearsed in the basement of a rooming house quite near town. The dances were coming along quite well. Steven and the dance company had the first three numbers blocked out, and they were making good progress on the music of the opening number. As they practiced, a number of people were watching from the street by putting their heads through the open basement windows. At the end of the evening, Steven asked one of the girls who was watching for a date the following Saturday in the early afternoon. Friday they had a rehearsal in the hospital auditorium, which was actually to be their home stage. They were, however, going to spend a lot of time on the road. Because his date was downtown the next day he stayed in the auditorium overnight. He slept in the wings of the theatre stage, right on top of some old discarded curtains.

Steven got up about eleven o'clock. He straightened himself around, and went out on the street to catch himself a Strässen Bahn. He got off at the street where the rooming house was situated. He walked up to the front of the house where he met the girl's mother just coming out of the hotel. The woman said that her daughter had to go to town with her father, and that he should come back another time. Steven felt a little disappointed.

He returned to the main street and headed for the Heidelberg shopping area up the Haüpt Strässe. There was a railroad track which crossed directly behind the hotel lobby, in which the parts for the show, had been assigned. Just as he arrived in sight of that track he saw a woman limping. She appeared to him to be the same woman he had seen from the lobby on Monday.

He was quite a long way away from her, and he was a little confused as to what he should do. He knew that he wanted very much to talk to her. At that moment she got on a Strässen Bahn. It didn't really matter to Steven where the Strässen Bahn was going, he got on, too. Right then he wanted more than anything to meet this woman. She appeared to Steven to be a bit too old for him, but perhaps she might know someone more his age.

The street car turned up the Haüpt Strässe just where Steven planned to go anyway. When the street car was about half way along its route the woman got up and got off right in front of a movie theater. She bought a ticket and then crossed street to an open air market.

Steven followed her across the street and said, "Entschuldigen bitte?" ("May I speak to you a moment?")

"Why are you bothering me? Because I limp?" she asked with a very thick German accent. She was a bit perturbed.

"No, you see, I had a friend back in the States by the name of Cynthia who had an artificial leg."

The lady smiled and said, "Oh, I see, well my name is Inge."

"My name's Steven, Inge, can I offer to buy you a drink? I'd like very much to talk to you."

"I just bought a ticket to the movie."

"Can I go with you?"

"No, don't do that. I'll meet you after the theater and we can talk then," she said. "I don't think that you would enjoy the movie, unless you can speak very good German. Can you?"

They walked over to the theatre and found out what time the movie would let out. Steven was ecstatic, as he walked up the strässe. He went into the Troubadour, a large gasthaus, just off the Haüpt Strässe, a few blocks from the theater. He had a couple of glasses of beer while waiting for the movie to be over. There was a juggler on stage. He wasn't very good.

"Oh, well, it's still only afternoon," he thought.

Steven had noticed that Inge did not walk well. She had a swing to her artificial leg as she walked. He wondered about the ace bandage wrapped around the ankle of her prosthesis. This did not matter at all to Steven. Steven understood about an amputee's walk, and that in itself made no difference. There were, indeed, more important considerations he had concerns about when he met an amputee. Steven was most interested in who each of these women really was. Steven believed that most of the women he met would be like Cynthia. Steven hoped to regain the lost piece. He wanted the power of inspiration that Cynthia had given to him, to be alive to him everyday through a woman like her. Steven's hope for this eternally renewed itself. He wondered if anyone could understand, if he told them. This was the first woman, since Cynthia, that he had met who at least had the physical attributes that Steven sought.

Steven was quite happy as he made his way down the street toward the theater and Inge. When he arrived at the theater, he found Inge waiting for him out front. Inge suggested that they go down the street to a quiet place where they could sit and talk. Steven ordered a glass of light wine for Inge, and a glass of Coke for himself. Steven knew that he had already had two beers, and he did not want to suffer the embarrassment of getting drunk in front of Inge.

They had a pleasant couple of hours together. They found talking together pleasant and easy. Steven and Inge started talking in earnest and she told him a great deal about herself.

"I was living in Berlin just after the war. I had lost my father and a much older brother during the war. I was living with my mother, and I had a small clerk job with the military in Berlin. One day I was crossing a field as a short cut to the laundry where I had my clothes cleaned. I was in a hurry and I barely heard someone yelling at me. I continued on my way, and the first thing I knew I felt a great pain. I fell to the ground and just laid there. I could not get up. I heard more than one shot ring out, and it felt like they all entered my left leg. I just laid there in pain. Soon an American soldier came over. He was the one who shot me, and he seemed to be very upset. He spoke to me, but at the time I knew no English. The guard summoned the corporal of the guard, and he got an ambulance to take me to the hospital. They sedated me and I didn't come to until the next morning. When I woke up, my left leg was gone. They had amputated it above the knee during the night. I was angry and frightened. I was very heavily sedated, which now I am thankful for, as the pain was excruciating when I finally was left without it. I found out what had happened to me a couple of days after I entered the hospital, I reached under my blanket and felt the wrapped end of my leg. The tears poured like rain down my cheeks. I could not believe it. Suddenly, I screamed at the top of my voice. I became frantic. I wanted to get up and run from the place, but I knew I couldn't. A sister came running in . . ."

"What's the matter?" she asked.

"What's the matter?" I replied. "Where is my leg?" I demanded.

"Bitte?" ("I beg your pardon?")

"I said, where is my leg, are you deaf?" I shrieked, in confusion.

The sister ran out of the room, in self-defense more than anything. She was obviously unprepared to give an answer to the question. In a few minutes a middle-aged man wearing a white coat walked briskly into the room. He saw Inge lying exhausted on the bed. Her face was completely covered with tears and beads of sweat covered her forehead.

"Was ist los? (What's going on?),'' he asked. "What is the matter?"

"My leg is gone!" The man who was her orthopedic surgeon slumped into the chair next to her bed and gently took her hand in his. He sat there silently for a long time. Inge seemed to calm down. He was at a loss, as he realized that Inge had no knowledge that there had to be an amputation. He could not blame her for her distress at the discovery.

He spoke, "Do you recall what happened two days ago?"

"There was a noise behind me, I felt a pain in my leg, and I fell. That's all I remember."

"You were hit five times in your left leg before you reached the ground!"

"What? Why did it happen? Could you not operate on my leg and take out the bullets?"

"No, unfortunately the bullets tore through your knee, destroying the bone and flesh in that area."

"Why didn't you tell me before you did such a thing to me. How could you do such a thing to me without telling me!"

"We had no way of waking you. Your life was on the line, and there was no possibility that your leg could be saved. If we hadn't taken your leg, you would be dead now! We had to make the decision for you, fraulein. I am, truly sorry."

"Shouldn't I have had the opportunity to decide whether I live or die?"

The doctor who had, in the course of time, treated hundreds of such patients, smiled slightly. "Inge, come to see me in a year's time, and then we can talk about it." He could only remember two of his patients who claimed that they would rather be dead, after having an amputation for a year. One of those actually committed suicide. "Believe me, that isn't you."

"Why me? What have I done to deserve this?"

"You didn't do anything to deserve it. It has been forced upon you. You will learn to make the best of it. Obviously you were unaware of the fact that the field was under heavy security. It was just your bad luck."

Inge paused a moment.

Steven shook his head. The pain he felt at her words could not be described. He said, "It must have taken you a long time to become cognizant of fact of what had happened to you."

"No, not really, although after all of these years I am not really used to the fact that I have only one leg. Right in the first few days, it seemed to me that my life was over. How would I ever get out of that bed. I was in the hospital for a month. Fortunately I didn't have any other wounds on my body. All of the shots entered my left leg. Before I left the hospital they got me up on crutches. I really had no desire to get up on crutches. I was crushed, and I could not imagine myself as I knew I now was. Steven, I have made the best of it. I'm married, and I have an infant baby boy at home. My husband just sold his architecture business in Wiesbaden."

Steven told Inge the whole story of Cynthia. Inge was quite impressed with the story of this young woman.

Steven queried "Do you understand why I might want to meet a young lady of my age similar to Cynthia?"

"Why, yes, I think that it might be easy to understand why you want to meet another woman like Cynthia."

"Do you, by any chance, know such a person?"

Inge lifted her glass to her lips to cover the little smirk that was coming upon them. "Let's see, a very sophisticated lady of about twenty years old?" she asked. "Uh, about five foot five?"

Steven nodded his head and grinned.

"Uh, perhaps blond hair?"

Steven nodded.

Inge frowned a playful frown. "And uh—one leg?"

"Yes?" Steven said.

"No, I don't think I know anyone like that!"

"Oh, nuts!" Steven said.

"She's a brunette!" Inge smiled.

"Really?" Steven beamed.

"It's not really all that simple. I'd have to have a talk with her."

"Would you? Oh, could you?"

"You know, I just might. Steven, you just might be a little

hard to explain to her," she said.

Inge gave Steven her phone number, and they agreed to meet on the next Wednesday. Steven rode with Inge until she got off of the streetcar. He proceeded to the auditorium, as he had no desire to return to Sechenheim that evening. He had a most pleasant sleep on the curtains.

Sechenheim, Monday. Steven and Ted, the other TDY soldier, assigned to special services for the show, were being given their orders by Captain Bradford, the special services military officer.

"You boys are to take your trucks to Mannheim and pick up a detail of men from the fifty-fourth tank battalion to move the folding chairs from Patton Barracks to the hospital auditorium. We are having Joseph Hinds, the renowned concert pianist in our area, for about a week. I can't tell you how important it is that everything goes smoothly for his visit. He will play at Patton, the hospital auditorium, and the auditorium theatre in Mannheim."

They picked up their trucks and headed for Mannheim. Steven picked up the troops and headed for Heidelberg. As he drove along the autobahn, he thought.

How would he ever be satisfied in regard to the many questions which Cynthia had inadvertently put in his head? He was thinking not only about the powerful living that Cynthia had shown him, which was one thing he was not sure where it could be found. It was that he was almost certain that things in life would never be right for him until he could experience the love of an amputee. This was difficult to tell anyone, but he knew it was the truth. He was glad that he had found Inge to talk to.

He knew the difference in their ages alone would prevent her from being that love that he sought. Perhaps, her friend, whoever she was, might be the woman. Perhaps, perhaps not.

Steven pulled the truck up to the hospital and the troops he had with him loaded the truck with chairs. They were traveling back and forth between Patton and the hospital. Finally at about 4:30, the hauling was finished. The troops loaded into the back of the truck. Steven hadn't had much of an opportunity to drive since arriving in Germany. He enjoyed driving, and right then he was on the autobahn, which had no speed limit. It had no speed limit, that is, for nonmilitary vehicles. The speed limit for military vehicles was thirty-five miles per hour. Steven found it frustrating driving on the autobahn at that speed. Just as soon as he pulled onto the off ramp that lead to the Mannheim-Kaserne exit, he floorboarded it full throttle. His foot no more than reached the floor when he heard a funny noise behind him. No, it wasn't a funny noise at all. It was the sound of a siren. He looked in his side mirror and, unbelievably, saw a brown car with an white star on the side and the unmistakable letters "MP." Steven eased his truck off onto the wide shoulder of the off ramp.

"DO YOU KNOW THE SPEED LIMIT ON THE AUTOBAHN!" boomed the MP.

"Ye - yes sir!" replied Steven.

"Well, what is it?" asked the MP, as he drew a long book out of his pocket and started to write.

"It's thirty-five, uh, sir."

"And how fast were you going, soldier?" he asked as he returned Steven's military I.D. to him.

"Forty-five, sir?" replied Steven, as he observed the big red "DR" on the top of the paper on which the MP had been writing.

"Not correct. Fifty and climbing. It's the climbing I'm writing you up for. Here this copy is for you. This next copy goes to your home unit in Karlsruhe. You'd better watch your ass, soldier."

Steven returned the boys in the back of the truck to their Kaserne, then headed, quite slowly as a matter of fact, for the Heidelberg Hospital Auditorium and the evening's rehearsal.

The rehearsals continued to go well. Erich and Jerry, the two directors, flew to London one evening to see a performance of *Wonderful Town*, which was currently playing there. They hoped to get some ideas for the show.

When the rules changes regarding getting laundry done,

Steven found it necessary to hang his washed underwear on the heater to dry. Well, between that and the fact that he was not required to be up and stand reveille with the other men, which met Steven was in the sack when the other men were shaved and gone, there were some complaints to Captain Bradford. Captain Bradford just mentioned the complaint to Steven and suggested that he take care of the matter.

Steven called Inge that afternoon, to verify their meeting. She said they should meet at the Cafe Oaise, which was a Gasthaus just about a mile down the street toward downtown Heidelberg, along the streetcar line Steven used going to and from the hospital. Steven agreed to meet Inge Wednesday at Seven. There was to be a late dance rehearsal at the auditorium, which was not to start until about 9:30.

When the stage crew work for the day was finished, at about 5:00, Steven rushed over to the medics barracks and talked one of them into letting him use their shower. There was no problem, so Steven took a nice warm shower, shook off the dust, changed into civilian clothes, and left his fatigues in one of the off stage rooms in the auditorium. He used his meal pass to eat at the hospital mess, and then he went out the hospital gate and started leisurely to walk toward the Cafe Oaise. He enjoyed the walk along the cobblestone street. The cafe was on the corner of a small street. It had a patio in front of it, which was surrounded by a high hedge, making it, the patio, quite a private area, away from the busy street in front of it. Steven moved up the three stairs which were in front of the entrance.

As he entered the room he saw Inge's back to him. She was seated with another woman. The other woman, who was facing him, had coal black hair, dark brown eyes, and a complexion which was in such contrast with her hair that it seemed to be as glistening snow. Steven was in the presence of one of the most beautiful women he had ever seen. Oh, could it be, he thought, that this beautiful woman is the one that Inge had spoken to of? But no, he could never come on such good fortune, or could he?

As Steven approached the table, the woman sitting across from Inge indicated with a facial expression, that she thought the one they were expecting might be nearing their table. Inge turned to look, smiled to her companion, and said very quietly to her, "Yes!"

As Steven came nearer, Inge turned to him, smiled, and said, "Steven, this is my very good friend, Herta, Herta Hausen. Herta, this is Steven Mack."

Herta extended her hand to Steven, which he took in a friendly German handshake. Herta had a book with her which she was studying. Herta told Steven that she was studying English at the English Institute, which was directly behind the Cafe Oaise, just down the hill.

Steven thought to himself that it was very possible this woman wanted to marry an American and go to the States. To Steven, that was an exciting thought. Steven actually thought that Herta, more or less, ignored him. Her being there sparked his interest, and really excited him. They spent an hour and a half together, and finally, Steven mentioned that he had a late rehearsal at the auditorium. The three of them agreed to meet on the following evening at the Gasthaus up the street.

As Steven got up to go, Herta got up at the same time. He walked behind her on the way out.

It was while following Herta out of the cafe that gave Steven an experience that he would never match in a life time. He knew that Herta had an artificial left leg. If he hadn't known it to begin with, he could not have guessed. Herta walked absolutely perfectly. The seams of her stockings were perfectly straight and in place. From out of her skirt, which came just below her knee, came a beautiful pair of legs coming perfectly to the ground. Steven took in what he saw in total disbelief and wonder. The beauty of what he had witnessed was a happening that he would not trade for a million dollars. He went with Herta to where she was to catch her streetcar, and then floated on air to the rehearsal.

Steven was in love. Oh, he just met her, but he knew. Oh what a beautiful lovely woman she was. Just to be near her. Steven's head was filled with beauty that night. The dance rehearsal went well, Steven felt as if he were flying. Some of the people who saw the rehearsal, thought he might be. This is the first time since leaving the States hat he had met someone that really peaked his interest. This person, in a way an opposite of Cynthia, really got to him. To him, Cynthia was power and guts; this woman was beauty and perfection. Perhaps, thought Steven, just perhaps, he had found the missing piece. That was a hope worth pursuing.

The stage work the next afternoon was lighter than usual for Steven. He had remained in the auditorium the previous night. There would be a late dress rehearsal that evening, and the show would open on Friday night. Steven changed once again into his civilian clothes and ate at the medics' mess at the hospital. A light rain had started to fall just about the time he started to eat. As soon as he had finished eating he started walking toward the cafe where they were supposed to meet. He began to worry about whether or not the girls would be there. He had obtained a pair of passes for the Saturday night's show from Mr. Rome. He had tucked them very carefully into the inside pocket of his jacket. As Steven continued down the street, he found that it was just raining too hard, and that he was going to arrive at the Gasthaus soaking wet. He took shelter in a doorway until a streetcar came along, and then hopped it. As the streetcar approached the restaurant Steven hopped off. He anxiously wondered if the girls would be there. He found, to his dismay, that would not remain a secret for long. As he ascended the stairs to the main room of the Gasthaus, he noticed that there were wet foot tracks leading up, but they were very uneven due to the prosthesis. The healthy leg left a very wet spot, while the prosthesis left almost none. Both ladies had above the knee amputations, so that they led their healthy legs up the stairs and pulled the others up to be even on the stairs. When Steven saw the patterns on the stairs he knew that they were both already in the Gasthaus.

They just sat and talked. Herta and Steven were drinking beer, and Inge was sipping her wine.

Steven queried them asking, "Would you ladies like to go to the show on Saturday night?"

They thought a bit. Inge said that it would be very nice to be able to see the show. Herta said she didn't really have another plan, so she thought it would be just fine. Steven agreed to meet them at the main gate of the hospital at 7:30 on Saturday. They had a nice evening together and parted until Saturday.

Steven was so pleased at how things were going with, not only one, but both girls. He looked back at what had happen over the past year and a half, and what was happening right now, he felt like he was the richest man in the world. Steven, at last, seemed to be headed in the direction he wanted. Perhaps the piece wasn't so lost after all. At any rate, things were coming up roses for him—for now.

Steven went to the gate at 7:30 Saturday evening, and was a little disappointed when he discovered that only Herta was there, and that Inge couldn't come. Herta explained that Inge had broken her leg, and it was in the shop for repairs. Steven took her into the theatre with him, and saw that she was seated before going back to the dressing room to prepare for the evening's performance.

As soon as the performance was over, Steven went down and collected Herta, and they left the theatre. Steven forgot about his clean-up duties, and figured it wouldn't matter for once. They rode out to Handshuseheim and found a quiet Gasthaus in which to have a drink. Herta recounted how much she had enjoyed the evening. She said she thought the show was excellent, considering that it was put on by nonprofessionals. They sat and talked for an hour or so and finally decided it was time to go home. They agreed to meet at the Platz at ten the next morning and go to mass together. Steven caught the streetcar and returned to the hospital auditorium.

The next morning Steven woke up bright and early, cleaned himself up, and met Herta for church. After church they took a walk down to the Neckar River. They were talking about the time, which would come, when Steven would return to the States. They were thinking of how nice it might be if they wrote to each other.

Then Herta said, "I am surprised that you have not asked

me about my leg to now?"

"I just felt that you would tell me about it when you felt comfortable about it. How it happened is not nearly as important as the fact that it did happen, and you are standing here with me now."

"We had been living in Heidelberg for three years. I was walking home from school one day with a girlfriend, when a car came over the curb and pinned me to the ground. My left leg was wrapped around the wheel of the car. But, the most frightening thing of all was that at that moment I was blind. Of course, it was only temporary, but I had no way to know it at the time. They took me to the hospital and sedated me. In the middle of the night I woke up in great pain. The doctor came in and examined my leg. He told me that gas gangrene had set in, and in the morning they would have to amputate. That was a shock. They sedated me again, and I knew nothing until I came out of the operating room. I was in the hospital for three months, and just before I was ready to leave, my crutches slipped on a highly polished floor and I fell and broke my arm."

Steven and Herta began to bond as two people who had a liking for each other on that day. But moving the relationship beyond that proved to be an almost impossible challenge for Steven.

It was seven, Monday morning at Sechenheim, when Steven was rudely awakened by the outside loudspeaker, which seemed to be calling his name for some reason. He was finally awake enough to realize that the speaker was demanding that he report to Captain Bradford immediately. This seemed strange to Steven, so he got dressed in a hurry and ran down to the special services office.

"You are to report to your commanding officer at Karlsruhe immediately!" stated Captain Bradford.

"I'm sorry, sir, I don't understand. Why does he want to see me?"

"Did you get a DR while driving that truck?"

"Yes, sir, I did."

"Well, you had better get your butt down there and get

things straightened out with him, if you can."

Steven left the captain's office, climbed into his truck, and headed for Karlsruhe, at precisely thirty-five miles an hour. Steven most assuredly did not want any more trouble. He had had enough to last him the rest of his stay in the Army.

It was nearly noon when he finally arrived at Neuröit Kaserne. He had posters advertising the play on each side of the truck. The show was to play in Karlsruhe within a few days.

He reported to the orderly room upon his arrival, and was told to go to his room and wait. He went to the radio operator's room to wait. He was greeted there enthusiastically by a couple of the other operators. They passed a pleasant half hour together, with Steven telling them about the show. Steven was keeping an eye out the window, toward the orderly room.

Suddenly the company clerk came out as though a bunch of wild horses were chasing him. Steven felt frozen in place. He knew that this was it. The clerk came up the stairs and into the room where Steven was. The clerk uttered but one word— "Mack." Steven followed the clerk down the stairs and into the orderly room. The clerk ushered Steven through the captain's door as the captain was closing his bottom drawer. He wanted to put his fingers in his ears, in anticipation of what was to come, but thought better of it.

"Oh, yes, Private Mack, I believe," the captain started. "Haven't we met before, wasn't it a few months ago? What the hell is this?" the captain asked, waving the DR report in Steven's face. "If I could arrange it, you wouldn't get a damn driver's license when you get out of the Army. Do you have any idea how much trouble you have gotten into while driving Army vehicles? Why, you alone have gotten into more trouble than the rest of the damn Army put together. This time I've got your ass. I am going give you something to remember me by, oh yes!" The captain had a slight smile on his face, as he said, "Mack, you're long over due for a court-martial! I think the time has come. I think we'll just do that. We'll relieve you of your entertainment duties. Maybe then you'll get it through your thick skull that this army is serious business. The court-martial will be tomorrow morning. You are confined to quarters until then. Now get your ass out of here.”

No one had made any mention of the fact that Steven had driven the truck down to see the captain to this point.

At eight o’clock the next morning, the captain had not yet sent for Steven. The phone on his desk rang. When he picked it up he found that he was speaking to Captain Bradford.

“I hope you will treat him decently.”

“I’m going to court-marshal the little bastard—before lunch!” replied Casey.

“He’s been doing a wonderful job in the show. We need him back! As a matter of fact I have a job that I need him to do this afternoon! If you’ll just send him back, I’m sure he won’t be any more trouble.”

“He’s the biggest screw-up I’ve ever had,” said Casey.

“You must admit, Casey that he is a pretty fine entertainer. He’s just young and immature. You should be a little more lenient with him because of his entertainer’s temperament.”

“He’s nothing but a big zero. If I send him back to the show, and he gets in some more of his idiotic trouble, I’ll see to it that both of your asses fry. Do you understand, Bradford?”

“Thank you, for your kindness, Captain. Good-bye.” Captain Bradford hung up the phone and put his head between his knees. He couldn’t remember when he had told so many lies. He really wanted to wash his mouth out. For him, it had a very bad taste. He thought, wait until I get my hands on that little bastard!

Captain Casey reached into the bottom drawer of his desk, and smiled at what he had in his hand from that drawer.

A few minutes later Steven was summoned to the orderly room. The company clerk informed Steven that he was to return to Sechenheim immediately. Steven put the truck on the autobahn. He was very glad that he had avoided the court-marshal, but could not imagine Captain Casey allowing him to go free. He knew that Casey had no love for him. He could not imagine Casey letting him go once he had him where he wanted him. Steven knew one thing, he would sure be glad to see

Captain Bradford once more.

As soon as he parked the truck, he went immediately to the special services office to report in to Captain Bradford, who was, for the moment his very hero. He was so glad to be back with the show. Captain Bradford's orderly ushered Steven silently into the Captain's office.

"Shut the door," the captain commanded gruffly. "First of all, let me see your driver's license. Steven took his driver's license out of his wallet and handed it to the captain, who took it with out taking his gaze from Steven. He took out his cigarette lighter from his pocket and incinerated the small piece of plastic. "I do believe that is the best use that either the lighter or the license has been put to. Now sit down! Do you know that, thanks to you, we don't have the use of the trucks any more. I suppose you think that I got you out of Karlsruhe because you are such an asset to the show. Well, that is hardly the truth. I was afraid that if Captain Casey found out what a boob you really are, that you might never get your butt out of the sling."

By this time, Steven was puzzled by what was going on. The captain seemed considerably more upset than Steven might have expected for just a speeding ticket. Steven was beginning to suspect that there must be something he was not seeing. He really began to wonder just what was going on.

Steven spoke. "Excuse me sir, but I don't quite understand what's going on here."

The captain looked at him in astonishment. "You don't understand? You don't understand! You, know—why I should be surprised at that. Well, let me tell you. First of all, I did not get you out of Neuröit just to be a nice guy. You, of course, know that your captain was going to give you a Summary Court for the speeding ticket you got, don't you? What do you suppose would have happened if he had known that you had stolen a truck?

"I beg your pardon, sir, a stolen vehicle?" repeated Steven.

"Who gave you permission to take that truck to Karlsruhe, anyway?"

Steven's face fell a mile, and for the first his mood turned grim. "Why, no one sir, I thought . . ."

"You thought? Yes, YOU thought! Because the vehicle was assigned to you, and you had to go to Karlsruhe, that you could just get in and go. Nice private transportation, hah! Well, while you were flying around Karlsruhe, The USARUA headquarters motor pool has been looking frantically for their stolen truck. The MPs have been looking for you. Now, do you wonder why I'm upset? Because of your stupid stunt, we no longer have any driving privileges. Do you have any idea, how we are going to move our equipment?"

"No sir, that was a stupid mistake. I am very sorry."

"Sorry? Just be glad that I got you out of Karlsruhe. If your captain, who I might mention, does not particularly care for you, had discovered that you had stolen the truck, it wouldn't have been a summary court-martial, but rather a general court-martial, and you probably would have had to do some hard time. Now do you see why I pulled you back here? To be sure, I have no love lost for you, but I see no intentional criminal act in what happened. You will continue in the show. If you don't screw up any more, I will consider any disciplinary action at the time the show is over. Oh, and before I forget, you will move to the hospital medics' barracks this afternoon. The company on this base will no longer tolerate you hanging your wash on their radiators. Is that understood?"

"Yes, sir, will that be all, sir?" queried Steven.

"Just one last thing, Mack, just one more time, just one more little mistake and you will wind up as a guest of the military prison system. You do understand! Don't you?"

"Yes, sir!" Steven returned to the barracks to pack. He packed up, caught a streetcar, and reported to the Heidelberg Hospital medics' quarters. He went to the show rehearsal that evening as if nothing had happened.

The show played twice more in Heidelberg, and then made it's brief road trip. They did one show in Karlsruhe, then went on to Bad Zollegen to entertain at a Canadian Air Force Base. They did two shows there and were wonderfully well treated. The base was near Baden-Baden. Steven took the opportunity to go over to where the famed casino was. He couldn't get in because he had no necktie with him. Baden-Baden was very plush little town and very green.

When the troop returned from Badden-Baden, Steven's three months were up and the show was over. Steven was to return to Neuröit Kaserne, and resume his "tough duties" as a radio operator. The afternoon, before he was due to depart, Captain Bradford summoned Steven into his office. When Steven heard what the captain had to say, he figured that the captain must have had his fingers crossed behind his back.

"Well, Steven, it has been a pleasure to have you as a member of our team. I only regret that it isn't possible for us to keep you here. Good luck with the rest of your time in Germany."

"Oh, yes, sir! Thank you, sir!" Steven replied.

The captain offered Steven a pleasant hand shake, and then Steven saluted the captain, as he left the headquarters his head was swimming to a point that he almost fainted. As soon as he was out of the captain's sight, he burst into laughter.

Steven had a dinner date with Herta that evening, so he hurried out to the hospital and changed his clothes. He picked up Herta in Hanshüscheim and they returned to Heidelberg to dine up on the side of mountain at the Mullkuncur. It was a very romantic place. They were served shish kebab on a flaming skewer. It was a lovely evening, and they danced together for the first time. Herta was able to dance a little bit.

Each one of them had a surprise for the other on Steven's final evening in Heidelberg. Herta told Steven that she was going to move closer to town in the next three weeks. She gave him her new address. Then Steven started to tell Herta what had been on his mind for a long time.

"I really don't know how to tell you this, I just want to say that I'm in love with you, Herta. You have made me care for you very much. Will you marry me?"

There was a very long pause, and Herta squirmed a bit in her chair, then said, "Steven, we are really such good friends, and I understand how you feel about me, but I don't love you."

"Why don't you love me? There isn't someone else is there?",

"Yes, there is. I should have told you sooner, but the occasion had not presented itself. I knew that you were falling in love with me, but I had no way to stop you. We have been having a lot of fun together, haven't we? I really didn't want to hurt you, but what can I say?"

Steven, feeling very sad, replied, "I understand, but it isn't easy. Steven really had to ask, "Tell me about him."

"His name is Han, and he is a air plane mechanic. He normally works in Bremerhaven, but currently he is in the States getting additional training. He will return to Germany in two months. Steven, you can come to visit me every week as soon as I have moved."

"Well, that's an awful lot better than if we were never to see each other again."

They rode the tram down the side of the mountain and caught the Strässen Bahn for Hanshüscheim. Steven and Herta said good-bye only with a handshake, and with the agreement that she would write to him as soon as she was settled. Steven returned to the hospital barracks, and the next morning caught the train for Karlsruhe. He was depressed at having to leave Heidelberg, and Herta.

When Steven returned to Neuröit Kaserne, he threw his tap shoes away. His once great ambition to become a professional actor had some how become dulled. He was almost certain now that he would study physical medicine and become a physical therapist. After he was back in Neuröit for about two weeks he received a note from Herta, inviting him to come up on the next Wednesday evening and visit her. Steven was very excited about the prospect of seeing Herta and her new flat. He took the streetcar from the Bahnhöf to Bismark Platz, and then walked across the new bridge to Herta's which was about two blocks on the other side of the river from Heidelberg. Steven walked down the narrow hallway, turned left up the three stairs, and rang the doorbell. Herta answered the door and, beaming all over, ushered him into what he took to be the living room. It was beautifully furnished with all new furniture. There was a sofa, a corner cabinet, and a dresser, all on a beautiful Persian rug. There were lovely new drapes, and a new chandelier.

Steven exclaimed, "What a lovely living room!"

"Oh, no this isn't only the living room, this is also my bedroom."

"It is really exquisite," Steven said.

Herta grinned with the pride and joy she had in her room.

The rest of the flat looked very much like the plain servants quarters to be found in a mansion. Her mother and her two brothers lived in the rest of the house.

Steven and Herta met together in her room a number of times. On one occasion, Steven told Herta about how much Cynthia had wanted to have a leg with which she could wear high heels. She had especially wanted it for her wedding. Herta was quite interested to hear about this because she had never heard of a woman in Germany, or anywhere else, wearing high heels with an artificial leg.

Two weeks later, when Steven came to visit her, she was wearing high heels. She looked terrific.

She told Steven, "I bought a pair of high heeled shoes, and took my spare leg to Herr Braun and told him that I wanted him to fix the foot, so that I could wear a pair of high heels. He looked at me as if I were crazy, but he did it. Herr Braun can't refuse me anything. When I put the leg on for the first time in his fitting room, I knew right away that it was going to be fine. I could walk better in the high heels than I could in low heels because the artificial foot required so little movement, and bending."

Steven said, "Wow! That's great! I think it's wonderful. It really does a lot for you."

The next time Steven came to visit her, they happened to be talking about limbs. On that occasion when, Steven realized that he had no idea what the knee on a prosthesis looked liked. He mentioned that fact to Herta as they were talking. As far as Steven could tell, Herta didn't make a move, but when he looked down at her skirt, her hem was above her knee and the knee, covered with an opaque stocking, was exposed.

"Would you like to see the leg?" she asked.

"Yes," he replied.

Herta got up off the couch, reached up her skirt, and undid her garter snaps on the left side. The snaps held both a regular nylon and an opaque, heavier stocking. She slipped the two stockings below her knee so that Steven could see her leg. The upper leg was made of wood, and was covered with a thin layer of leather. The lower leg was the same. Her ankle was stiff, because she preferred it that way. The knee was hinged, but when covered, it appeared much as a normal knee. There was no one in the world who knew more about wearing a prosthesis than Herta. Herta taught Steven a great deal about artificial limbs, but little about love.

Steven went to Heidelberg every week to visit with Herta. It was always in his heart that perhaps something would change in their relationship. It was never evident that anything did. When Han returned to Bremerhaven, Herta went to be with him for a week. That Christmas, Herta invited Steven to spend Christmas Eve with her family. It was a lovely evening. They walked across the Nekar River on the new bridge. The frozen river glistened in the full moonlight.

Steven and Herta never left the house during these visits. They became well acquainted, and he learned a great deal about the problems of amputees. He fell even deeper in love with Herta. Herta told him just about everything she could about herself.

The visits went on and nothing was changing, so Steven offered to take Herta any place she would like to go in Europe on his leave. She said that if she were to accept such an offer, she would choose Rome. He agreed, and she promised to write him in a few days, with her decision.

During the next week, Steven received a letter from Herta telling him that she would not be able to make the trip with him. A few weeks later, during their visit together, they decided not to meet any more because it was becoming too difficult, as love was just not bringing them together.

The piece was still missing. The piece he lost in Missouri, was still gone. He had the hope, for a while, that at last he had found someone who could fill the void, but alas, it was not to be. Steven returned to Neuröit and laid on his bunk and wept for three days.

Finally, Captain Casey summoned Sergeant Rameriz to his office.

"Well, Sergeant, what the hell's the matter with the little bastard now?"

"Sir, I'm not to sure."

"Well, he sure as hell can't lay around like that. Oh, shit!"

"I think it has to do with a girl in Heidelberg."

"I knew it, I should have never let him go to Heidelberg in the first place."

"I guess he's a bit love sick?"

"A bit? That's putting it mildly, Sergeant. I can't believe this shit. Don't we all have woman trouble at times, Sergeant?"

"Yes, sir"

"I notice that most men manage to carry on their work with little obvious trouble, don't they? Why don't you take him out and get him laid?"

"I don't think it would do any good, sir."

"The reason that I called you, Sergeant, is because I think that we should send Private Mack to Kaiserslautern for a psychiatric exam, and I wanted your input."

"I think that you have a good idea, sir. Perhaps, they'll be able to help him."

"Perhaps, they'll lock him up, and we'll be rid of the little bastard! We may as well be optimistic hadn't we, Sergeant. So, it's settled. You may go, Sergeant," said the captain with a strangely familiar smile.

The sergeant saluted Captain Casey, and left the room. When he was gone, the captain reached into his bottom desk door, pulled out a half empty fifth of bourbon, and poured a double shot into his half empty coffee cup.

Steven went to Kaiserslautern for a series of psychological tests. Steven never found out how the test came out, except that he had one more interview in regards to the testing at the Heidelberg hospital. They sent him back on his job, saying that he was able to work, even though he was showing some signs of depression. One incident occurred while he was at Kaiserslautern which Steven never was sure about.

He went out on pass the night that he was there. After he went to bed, he woke up in the middle of the night, only to realize that someone had their elbow in his groin. When he gained his senses he recognized that it was the sergeant who had administered his tests that day. Steven removed the sergeant's hand. They talked for a while about the previous day's activities, and the sergeant left. Steven was never quite sure if this was a part of the tests, trying to determine if he had any homosexual tendencies, or if, indeed, the sergeant had such tendencies.

There were only three more occasions on which he got into little scrapes. The first was when he got into a card game with a couple of Germans in a Gasthaus in Karlsruhe. The three of them were drinking, or so it would seem. They were playing a German gambling game, which Steven enjoyed very much. Apparently, Steven was not drinking the same stuff as his opponents. At any rate, Steven picked himself out of the middle of the street an hour or so later, with no memory of what had happened. His wallet was gone, and of course, his picture of Cynthia. He was carrying what was probably the most cash he had ever carried to town, as in the past week he had had his only winning streak. At any rate, somebody from his unit found him on the street and saw to it that he got back to the barracks.

There was a second time when he arrived at the guard shack completely soused. For some reason he had a bit of an argument with the guard. The guard did not particularly want to argue, so he arrested Steven and kept him in the guardhouse over night.

It was during this period, of not being in contact with Herta, that the third occasion occurred. Steven decided to try to talk to Inge about his problem with Herta. He wrote a letter, proposing a meeting on a Saturday in Heidelberg. When he called Inge on the phone Saturday, he was informed that she was out. He continued to call throughout the day. He went to town in the early afternoon and started drinking, as he continued to try to contact Inge. By eight that evening, Steven was very drunk and crying bitterly. The MPs picked him up, and after talking to him for quite a long time returned him to the Kaserne. Steven missed seeing Herta greatly. He longed to go to her, but he knew that she would not see him.

It was now nearing the time that he would be returning to the States. Steven went to Old Neuröit quite frequently in these days. He had found a young boy, who had only one leg, riding a bicycle. Steven made some inquiries about the boy at the Gasthaus that he hung out in when he was in the village. He made arrangements to meet the boy, and talk to him. After talking to him, Steven decided to buy him his first artificial leg. The boy had lost his leg during a bombing raid, while he was in his house. It happened on his birthday. Steven went to Heidelberg to see Herr Braun. They agreed, providing that Fritz's stump was in a condition that he could be fitted, and Steven made an appointment with Herr Braun. The price, at that time, was less than two hundred dollars, and the leg was to be of the very best quality.

The following Thursday afternoon, Steven arrived with fifteen-year-old Fritz at Herr Braun's. He examined Fritz, and said that, even though Fritz had had a very crude amputation, he could be fitted. Steven left Fritz with Herr Braun. He walked to the new bridge across the Nekar and went to Herta's house. She invited him in, and they had a long visit. He told her about Fritz. She said that she would like to meet the boy, so after he went back to Herr Braun's shop, he took the boy to Herta's house. Steven found out later that Herta was not pleased. She knew that such war injuries were taken care of by the government. She speculated that the boy's father had spent the money. This didn't matter at all to Steven, because he was so pleased to be able to help the boy, and see him with two legs. Not only could Fritz ride a bicycle, but he was also a member of the town's gymnastics team. His parents were poor. Fritz was an apprentice to a costume jewelry maker. His future really did not look bright.

Steven was sleeping in, one Saturday. As he woke he could hear some of the other operators talking about Fritz, and the fact that Steven was getting him a leg. In the midst of the conversation, a big, burly operator stood up in the floor to tell us of his misfortune. When he was sixteen years old, he broke his leg playing baseball. It happened just before summer vacation and he was unable to play all summer. He was almost in tears as he told the story. He was full of self pity. No one in the barracks said a word, but they really passed the looks around. They could not figure out what kind of mentality this man had. Maybe they felt sorry for him.

Steven had only a few weeks left in Germany. His entire unit was being rotated home and Steven would be discharged two months early. Herta and he visited together often in those last few weeks. There was no romance, but a friendship each of them enjoyed. Before Steven left Germany, he attained the rank of specialist third class. It was a new rank with pay equivalent to a corporal. This was as high a rank as Steven had seen anyone attain with three years of service.

He also received the good conduct metal. The captain presented it to him, in a special ceremony. He told Steven that he presented the medal personally because he really didn't think Steven was getting it, and wanted to see Steven's name on the certificate that came with it. All he said as he pinned it on Steven was, "Oh, shit! I suppose that they'll be passing these out in Leavenworth next."

One of the other operators said that he was going to give his back. Steven had never really been court-marshaled, and the only way to lose the medal was to face a court. He seemed to understand the captain's sentiments. In Steven's case, it was not good conduct, just dumb luck.

On Steven's last trip to Heidelberg, Steven and Herta laid together on her sofa bed and talked about their separate plans. He enjoyed the evening with Herta, but he was very sad to be leaving her. They talked together for a long time, and Steven proposed to her, one more time. When it came time for Steven to leave, they kissed for the very first time.

It was Steven's very last week in Germany. He had supper with Isabelle one last time. He knew that Isabelle liked him a lot, but also knew she was not the woman for him, even though they almost went to bed that last night. Finally, he went to Fritz's house one evening. They always had a wine cider drink for him. Fritz had taken his new leg home with him two weeks before. Steven came by on many occasions to help Fritz with learning to walk with the new leg. Steven had to leave too soon to be any real help with teaching Fritz how to walk. That night Fritz's parents gave Steven a ceramic bird, to thank him for what he had done for Fritz.

ROTATION DAY! Three deuce and a half's rolled through the gates of Neuröit Kaserne loaded with their replacements. What a sight to see. Troops were all over the place, with only one reason to be there, to send Steven and his unit home. The radio network was still in tact. It had been in operation for the whole time. Specialist Third Class Steven Mack was given the duty of turning the network over to the new operators. There wasn't much to it, but Steven felt some how honored.

The battalion boarded the busses and head for the waiting train out in the middle of nowhere. They boarded it and started their trip to Northern Germany, and Bremerhaven. There were five radio operators returning with the rotation, and all but one was being discharged. They took up one compartment in the train. They enjoyed each others' company for the whole way home. Steven was very surprised when the train did not go through Heidelberg. He was disappointed, and perhaps a little relieved. Steven thought that if the train had stopped in Heidelberg, it wouldn't have taken much to get him to jump ship and go to Herta just one more time.

Soon Steven settled back in his seat next to the window, thinking about all those things that had happened in the last three years, and about the two years he spent in Germany. He had not practiced his religion as he knew he ought to. With no excuses for himself, he didn't see many that did. He had been with a couple of prostitutes while he was there. He just felt a bit hypocritical. He took up with Isabelle because she was a Catholic, and he wanted to treat her with respect. Steven only found what he really wanted in Herta, and she was still crushing his heart.

Steven was pretty well certain that once he returned to the States he could get right with God and continue his confession of faith within the Catholic church. He had a love for the church. He had a great desire to learn. He had wanted to have a college degree for as long as he could remember. No one in his family had one. Now, with his G.I. bill money he felt that he would, within a few short years, have it.

His mind turned to Herta. She hadn't gotten married, and he hadn't seen a man around her during the year that he knew her. Why had he failed with her? She might have been able to provide the missing piece, but as it was, she left him more empty than ever. Why didn't she at least go to bed with him once, so that he could know how it might have been to make love to her?

The train pulled into the embarking area at Bremerhaven, The troops got off the train and in a seemingly endless line disappeared into the ship.

There was no question! None whatsoever. The piece that he had lost to Cynthia was still missing, and Steven had no idea how he might find it! Perhaps he never would. Could it be that she was its only keeper?

Section Three:
Herta II:
Herta in America

There is a time to settle and a time to move
There is a time to be apart and a time to be together
There is a time to part to part to part
Until the empty room is no longer empty but filled
with tears.
There was time to stop, to stop even hope.

I went from the ecstasy and joy of being with to Herta to the sorrowful thought that I would never see her again. For whatever the reason, I was almost destroyed. The piece was totally beyond my grasp. Now Herta in America . . .

The USS *Buntner* was on the last day of its voyage. Steven had packed his gear and was standing on deck, with the strap of his duffel bag firmly in hand. The ship would soon dock at the Brooklyn Navy Yard. The excitement that he felt was beyond description. There was a certain pride that suddenly rose within him that morning. It was a pride in being an American. It was a pride in being home. Even though there was no war when he left, and even though he was young when he left, there was that unrealistic fear that he might never come home again. He had never realized, until this very moment, how thrilled and exhilarated he would feel to be home again. There was more, much more. The greatest thing of all was that his father was still alive. He had held such fear that his dad would not survive until he got home, but he did. Steven stood on the deck and leaned over the rail. All the guys on top deck were watching something. It was a school of whales in view about a half mile from them. The whales' water spouts could be seen shooting into the air.

The Statue of Liberty came into view not long after that. That was a dear sight indeed. It was not until Steven had docked at the Brooklyn Navy Yard and the order was given to debark that the tears broke loose and covered his face. They came off the ship and directly onto a waiting bus. He was going home.

It took three days to cross the country. Finally they got off the train in Southland. Steven called his grandmother, who lived in Southland, to let her know that he as home. Steven, and the other boys with him, boarded the Pacific Coast Day Light. It was the same train Steven had seen stop numerous times at the train station in Grape Arbor. The train was bound for Fort Ord.

The trip along the ocean was enjoyable and relaxing. Steven

remembered he had a cousin who lived just a few short steps from where the train would stop at Grape Arbor. When the train stopped, Steven charged off the train and ran around a blind corner. He almost knocked his mother over. It was quite a meeting. They threw their arms around each other and cried for joy at seeing one another. Steven's grandmother had called his mother and told that he was coming. She provided him with the surprise of his life. They had a two or three minute visit and then Steven climbed back on board the train. This was a surprise, but he already knew that his father was going to meet him.

When they got off the train in Salinas, a bus was waiting to take them to Fort Ord. As the bus stopped at the replacement center, he saw his father and stepmother parked in their car directly across the street from where the bus stopped. Steven, once again excited, raced across the street to greet them. He was so pleased to see his father alive, and thankful to God. He spoke to them for a few moments and then went to report in. The guys were all told where they could stow their duffel bags. As soon as he had done this, he discovered that everyone's passes were made out and that they did not have to return until six A.M. the fifth of July.

He returned to the car and, after two long years, he spent a wonderful few days with his father at home. Steven rode back to Fort Ord on the bus and started thinking about his dad.

His father was in the hospital when Steven graduated from high school. It was the first operation for his ulcer condition. Steven and his family were all very excited because there had been a high degree of success with this particular operation. Unfortunately, peritonitis set in after the operation. He laid near death for days. Steven was at the hospital near midnight, one evening, when his father stated that he wanted a priest. That was a surprise to Steven, because, as far as he knew, his dad did not believe. He did not know whether or not his father was rational at the time. At any rate, he ran over to the cathedral, which was nearby, as quickly as I could. It was the first time he ever heard his father mention wanting to talk to a religious person. Steven rang the doorbell at the rectory, waited a few minutes, and rang again. There was no answer! He waited and rang some more. Finally, he started pounding on the door and shouting

"ANSWER THE DOOR! My father is dying! He needs you, please answer please!" Almost exhausted, he broke into tears. He could fight no longer. It was no use, no one gave a damn.

By some miracle, Steven's dad survived the operation. He came home, and went back to work driving truck, but he never fully recovered from the operation.

Steven stepped off the bus, walked to the edge of town, and hitchhiked to the fort, not wanting to wait for the next bus. After eating on the base, he decided to go over to a little town, which was only a very few miles from the base, one last time. He went out the gate, without bothering to pick up his pass, and hitched a ride over. After having a few beers at a little bar, he gave some thought to tomorrow. It was going to be the biggest day of his life. He was going to get his discharge. That was for sure. In case, you didn't know, Steven hated the Army with a passion. Tomorrow was the day all good non-soldiers looked forward to most. Steven, right now, was on top of the world.

At eleven A.M., July 5, 1956, Steven Mack, having completed two years, ten months, and nineteen days, exited the main gate of Fort Ord—never, NEVER to return. He had gotten the promotion of his lifetime to PFC—Poor F--king Civilian.

Steven went to Grape Arbor to see his mother. The bus trip took a couple of hours. He napped a while, then he remember that which he could never forget. He wished he could forget but . . .

Steven was eight when, one afternoon he came home from school and nobody was home. This wasn't the first time it had happened. By then he knew, instinctively, why no one was home. He tried to deny the facts to himself, but down deep he knew. It had happened again. He tried to busy himself with playing his record machine and looking at his old comic books, but it was no use. Finally he called his father at work. He was crying by the time his father came on the line. It reassured him to hear his voice.

"Just calm down, son, I can't leave right now. There are a couple of things I need to finish before I can come home. Find something to eat in the kitchen, and I'll be there as soon as possible."

"Thanks, Dad, but please hurry! It's lonesome here."

"Yes, I know, son, I've got to go now."

Steven went out to the kitchen, made himself a little sandwich, drank some milk, and ate a banana. Normally he would be across the street playing with the neighbor kids, but this was not a normal time. He had experienced this before and it was no pleasure. Finally, after what seemed like hours, his father made it home.

"Let's go find her, Dad. I want my mother!"

"Yes, we will, but first, have you eaten, son?" Dad asked.

"I had a jelly sandwich, a glass of milk, and a banana." He pulled at his Dad's hand and said with urgency, "Let's go Dad, let's find Mama." He tugged harder.

His Dad pulled him closer to him and said, "Okay, let's go."

They went to town, and Dad stopped the car and went into one bar after another. Each time he came out almost immediately. Finally, he went into a bar and didn't come out for a long time. Steven knew that she was in there. When he did come out, she was not with him.

Steven asked, "Was she there?"

He could see that Dad was almost in a rage when he said, with anger in his voice, "She's very drunk, son, let's get out of here."

As Dad pressed the starter of the car. Steven opened the door, pleading, "I want my Mama, I want my Mama." He ran to the bar,

"No, Steven, come back!" His father shouted, but he was already two steps from the door of the bar.

He entered, and spotted his mother immediately. He ran over to her and stood looking up at her on the bar stool. "Mama, I'm here!" he said, as he tugged gently on her coat.

She turned and looked down, her every mannerism so familiar to him. She acted completely different when under the influence of alcohol. When she looked at him, she appeared to be very sad. It was a look that said, "I know I failed in my responsibilities, but I had to." He understood the meaning of his mother's look only much later in his life.

She said, "Go home, baby, you mustn't be here so late at night. Where is your father?"

"Come on, Mama, let's go home!" he pleaded through bitter tears. "Please, let's go. Mama, I need you so much, please. Daddy is waiting for us in the car. We need you Mama! Please!" Steven was crying quite loudly by then, and luckily his mother was becoming embarrassed by his presence.

"Where's your father?" she asked, as she took him by the hand and left the bar.

When they reached the car, she inquired, "What the hell are you doing letting the kid come into a bar?"

"He ran in before I could catch him. Come on, get in the car, and let's go home."

"I'm never coming home, Mr. Mack! I can't take you anymore. I've got to go. Just leave me alone!"

As his mother was saying this, Steven was pulling on her skirt, crying and begging her. Finally, she noticed his tugging and in the midst of the rage, she looked down and put her hand gently on his head and rubbed it. She took his hand, got into the back seat, and pulled him gently against her breast. It was a silent ride home.

When they got home, his Dad told him to go to bed, and his mother and dad went to their room. As he went to bed, he was worried about his mother. She drank frequently, and at his young age, he really believed that she was killing herself. He thought that if she didn't quit drinking, she would soon be dead.

About that time he heard a terrible racket in the other bedroom. It was his mother and father arguing. It began to sound more and more violent. Suddenly his mother came into his bedroom, without a stitch of clothes on, his father right behind. His mother climbed into bed with him and huddled up to him.

It was then that he noticed that his father, dressed only in his shorts, was carrying his belt. He pulled the covers off of them and started beating his mother. It was a terrible experience for all of them.

The bus pulled into a station for a rest stop. After an exchange of passengers, the trip resumed. Steven thought about some of the things behind these happenings which he had not learned of until many years later.

At that time, Steven was totally on his father's side because, after all, it was his mother who was deserting him. She was the one that went off to get drunk. He had also seen her near other men. What Steven didn't know about his mother was that she had caught his father in a sex act with another woman. Steven also didn't know that his father was beaten almost to death with a buggy whip, by his mother, when he was a boy. After hearing about that, he knew why his father told him never to let a woman hit him. He didn't understand that the first time he heard it. Even so, he always believed that he could never strike a woman.

His mother had remarried while he was in Germany. The man she had married was a department store manager. He had two young daughters. That was all Steven knew about him.

As the bus pulled into the station in Grape Arbor, he could see his mother standing nearby with her new husband. He grabbed his duffel bag, and stumbled off the bus. He threw the bag on the ground, put his arms around his mother, and gave her a big hug and kiss. When it was over, he shook hands with his new stepfather, Ed. They all got into the car and rode the few blocks home.

Steven felt so free now that he was out of the Army. The only problem was that he was very much in love with Herta. He cared a great deal for her, perhaps as much as he did for Cynthia. The difference was, that his loss of Cynthia was a total loss. That relationship, he knew, never got its start and he knew it never would. The one that had taken the piece would never be able to return it. Now with Herta, well, perhaps there was hope that she might in some manner fill the hole. He didn't believe that this would happen, either. After all, Herta could never bring herself to tell him that she loved him. There he was with the missing piece. He became quite depressed at times. At other times he felt good and was full of energy.

Steven and Herta had agreed to write to each other. Steven wrote his first letter to Herta while he was still at Grape Arbor.

For him, it was a relaxing time. It was a full two weeks of vacation, the first in sometime. He had taken only one short leave, of a week's duration, while he was in Germany. He tried to save the leave time so he would have that much more money for school.

There was a little beach just south of Grape Arbor where he first learned to body surf when he was a teenager. His mother lent him her car so that he was able to go swimming on several occasions.

One Saturday night, his mother lent him her car again, and he drove to another little beach town to attend the Saturday night dance. He met a girl named Carole at the first dance he attended that summer. She was a short Italian girl with black hair, and large engaging eyes. She was from a nearby town. She was Steven's age and a college senior studying to be a teacher at a college in the southern part of the state. The following week, they met again at the dance. After it was over, they went down to the beach. They left their shoes at the bottom of the stairs that led to the beach, and had a perfectly wonderful stroll through the sand and shallow surf. Steven and Carole liked each other's company very much. From these meetings they formed a friendship which was lasting. Steven had the feeling that she could have been serious about him, but frankly the time for that possibility was over when he met Cynthia.

After Steven met Cynthia, his mind was set on marrying an amputee. Whether it was Cynthia, who became an amputee so that she could have the abundance of life she craved and justly deserved, or Herta whose beauty and vanity drove her to walk so well that no one could say that she had a missing limb, or some other amputee, he knew that he must find one. He had to experience life with a person who had lost a limb. Why? Was it the way Cynthia revealed herself to him in great power and zest for life? Was it the beautiful, apparent normalcy of Herta? Was it perhaps Inge's raw courage? Was it looking forward to the experience of seeing his wife in the bedroom and enjoying her nudity as much as any man could? Was it experiencing her nude body against his in their bed? Steven's fantasy led him to believe that all of these were true. Steven could see no handicap in any of them. Yet, it was still a deep mystery to Steven. He thirsted for the right handicapped woman. He doubted that he would ever find her. Steven had a long history of not having the things he most wanted in life. Would this also be a never realized dream? It was one that he must unravel.

After the two weeks were over, Steven decided it was time to return to Central Valley. He took the opportunity to think about his immediate future, especially school. Steven had always wanted to go to college. He was never sure what his major would be until he met Cynthia. By that time he realized that he wanted to be in a position in which he could really do something for handicapped people. He was seeking the most satisfaction that he thought he could get from his life's work. He wanted to be a physical therapist. The excitement of the thought of actually starting college held him awe struck.

Dad had invited him to stay at home while he was going to school. It was a wonderful gesture on his father's part. There really was no question about accepting the offer after it was made. Steven had saved almost two thousand dollars in bonds, leave pay, and his mustering out pay. Both his mother and his father had promised to give him a car when he got out of the service. The car his dad was going to give him was a Nash Coupe of about 1950 vintage. It was wrecked on a trip to Southland. The Ford, which had been promised him by his mother, was still in the yard when he left town. He supposed that his stepfather had put his foot down, or that there was some sort of squabble over it.

It was very hot crossing the valley at that time of year. Thankfully, the heat of the valley was unlike the heat of the Midwest. It was a dry heat in the valley, and it cooled off considerably in the evening. Unlike the Midwest, at night, a blanket was required in order to stay warm and sleep. Nevertheless, IT WAS HOT!

Many times, while still in high school, Steven made the trip across the valley to spend summer vacation with his mother. At that time, his mother was married to a bus driver. These visits were fun time for him. His stepfather taught him to drive in an old Model-A. He took Steven and a couple of his buddies to the beach two or three times a week. He generally had fun when he was at his mother's for the summer. She had a very good job, but her life style, especially her drinking, was very difficult for him to cope with. Therefore, he always returned to Central Valley to continue in school.

Steven settled back for a pleasant trip home. He would at last settle in his home. Right now that was a pleasant feeling. He remembered riding through the thick fog at night, with his father, in his truck . . .

"Thanks, Dad, for giving me a chance to work with you."

"That's all right, son, I like to have you along when my regular helper isn't able to come. Besides, I knew you could use the twenty-five bucks."

"I sure can, I only make seventy-five cents an hour as soda jerk at the drive-in and I'm working four to eleven because of school. Gee, Dad you'd better wipe the windshield, it's getting hard to see."

"Wiping the windshield isn't the answer, son," came the reply.

Steven's Dad turned on the wipers. It helped but little. They could barely see beyond the front end of the truck. "Here look at this," his dad said. He reached over and switched the lights on high beam for a few seconds. The lights turned the fog a bright white and almost blinded them.

"Dad, this is really dangerous! How are you able to come out here all the time?"

"I've got to make a living. We live in this valley and trucks are my livelihood. Just last week, there was a one-hundred car pile up. Three people were killed. Do you know what the most dangerous thing is about this fog?"

"The fact that you can't see anything beyond the truck?"

"No, not really. The most dangerous part is that there are some idiotic maniacs out there that don't understand that you have to slow down. They breeze along a sixty or sixty-five miles, and annihilate some poor bastard nervous about driving twenty-five miles an hour. These things happen all the time. The one thing that gives me some peace out here is the size of this truck!"

"Yeah, I guess you're right, Dad"

Steven and his father delivered two full trailers of produce and groceries. The produce wasn't difficult, but they had to pick up the cases of can goods and put them on a roller conveyer belt. Those cases were heavy . . .

The bus pulled into the Greyhound station in Central Valley. Steven's stepmother met him at the station. His father was already at work, driving his truck on the northern run to pick up another load of groceries and produce. In a few minutes he was home, home for good. Steven went into his bedroom and threw himself across the bed in a private triumph of having survived the very worst.

Steven's father was a tough S.O.B. As near as he had come to dying, and as sick as he still was, he continued to let that truck jiggle his guts. Steven knew that it was a hell for him, but he also knew that his pride in taking of care of his responsibilities would not let him quit. He was basically a good man and everyone really loved him. He could never find peace in himself.

He came home about midnight, with the traditional bunch of bananas from the truck in his hand. Steven and his father sat around and talked in the living room for a couple of hours before they turned in. Steven just loafed around for a few more weeks, and finally decided to go to work. The time to register for school was several weeks away. Steven was trained as a cook, a wireman, a radio operator, and a driver. He was convinced that he didn't want to be caught dead behind a hot stove. He knew of no wire trucks that he could chase. There was almost no such thing as a professional Morse Code operator. That left driving. Steven sure as hell couldn't drive a big rig, so he decided to take a job with the local taxi company. Fortunately, the taxi company did not have his driving record from the Army. That was probably lucky for him, as the taxi chief, seeing that Steven had just been discharged, was more than happy to hire him.

Steven worked for the cab company for a little over a year. He worked full-time during the summer, fifty hours a week, and part-time while he was at school, nights for forty-eight hours a week. Sometimes he was able to study in the cab. Many stories have been written about cab driver's over the years. Only a very few will be related here. Make no mistake about it, cab driving was one hell of an adventure for Steven.

The average driver, this was in 1956, earned a dollar an hour plus tips. Most cab drivers were poor and uneducated. Some of them were seriously physically handicapped. Most of the drivers, there a few women even at that time, couldn't get another job. Many of them were married with families. It was a tough life for them. Some of them, mostly the ones who worked nights, were involved in bootlegging, and prostitution. They bootlegged by keeping bottles of booze in their trunks for after hours sale. One of Steven's friends who was driving a cab, by the name of Fred, had just moved to the west coast. He was to be a professor at state college when school started in the fall. He was a drama teacher.

It was a tough time, to be sure, for Steven, but he was able to save all of the checks he received under the G.I. bill. He still held hope that Herta might decide to marry him.

School started, and through Fred's kindness, Steven was allowed to take public speaking during his first semester. He also took German. The first day of class, to his surprise, a fellow who left the same field observation battalion in Germany about the same time that he arrived there was in his class. Another one of his buddies, who happened to be a native of Germany, and went through basic with him, was also at school.

Because of his depression and anxieties, seemingly all over Herta, Steven was convinced before he had completed his psychology class that he had some sort of mental malady. His professor seemed to be convinced of it also. If he knew what the diagnosis was, which Steven doubted, he did not say. Steven thought that psychiatry and accurate diagnosis seldom met. He thought that the reason for this might be that the various patients psychiatrists see really slip over lines of illnesses, and actually show evidence of more than one illness at various times. If you asked one, he would probably admit to it.

There was an occasion when he felt so bad that he made an appointment with a counselor at school. When she called him in, he went into her room, put his head on her desk, and cried for fifteen minutes. When he stopped crying he left the room without ever having said a word.

Steven enjoyed his first year back at school, he especially enjoyed his history teacher, Michael Boyd. Professor Boyd was a man of about sixty He called Steven into his office because he failed the first test in his class, and Professor Boyd had his doubts as to whether or not Steven would make it in college. The first year of college has a terrific turn over rate. They talked and Professor Boyd gave him some very good tips on studying. These tips enabled him to succeed. The class was, of course, a freshman requirement, History of Civilization. This was, without a doubt, one of the most significant classes Steven ever took. In the course of this class, the history of the Roman Catholic church was explored. According to Steven, the corruption of the church, in those days, was beyond belief. How could this church be so corrupt and still claim to be the one true church? In light of this corruption, how could they really expect anyone to follow their teachings? Professor Boyd and Steven had some very rich discussions on this matter. Steven reflected that if the Catholic church was not the one, then which one was. Steven could see none. Steven went to visit with a Catholic priest one afternoon. Shortly after that, he quit the church. He felt more certain, through the history book, that Jesus had indeed lived, but that did not solve the entire problem. His great problem, about religion, which he no longer actively practiced, but rather took a wait and see attitude, was the definition of the word "church." It took a very long time for him to receive the answer to that question.

Steven went to school on Monday, Wednesday, and Friday. This made it possible for him to put in a good number of hours driving the cab.

His freshman class decided to put on show for the rest of the student body. Steven had an idea and put an ad in the *Daily Goat*, the school newspaper. The ad asked for freshman students, who would like to dance, to come to a tryout. He needed four males and four females. He got exactly the four couples he needed. In the final portion of *Wonderful Town*, there was a dance routine called the "Vortex Ballet." It had a slow, haunting melody. The four couples were on a three foot platform. During the course of the dance the couples danced off the platform to the stage. Of Steven's eight dancers, only one had any dance experience, and Steven had never done any choreography before. The project was to be completed in time for the show, three months down the road. He was about three years older then the rest of the kids. They were a wonderful bunch, and they stuck together through the entire three months. They gave a fine performance, and grew to work together very well.

In the course of the three months, he came to be in charge of the entire show. He got himself in trouble, or at least made himself a bit unpopular. The reason being that he had been working with his group for three months, and they knew him. The rest of the cast came on board for only a few days before the show went on. Steven planned for a finale with the entire cast. In trying to work it out, he became a bit angry, and started hollering. That was all right with his little dance group because they knew him. At any rate, his display of anger seemed to alienate him from the large cast. The show came, and it was a success, but before the night was over, Steven was drunk and depressed. He had no comfort in the attitude of the cast or his success of that evening. He had failed, as he had so many times in the past, to make friends as he really wanted to.

There were a couple of things which happened to him, while driving cab, that must be mentioned. His object in driving cab while going to school was to get enough money to be able to support Herta, if he ever managed to get her to come to the States. One evening, as he was driving down the street, a man in his early fifties hailed him. There were two men talking to him. They were trying to get him to get into a car with them. He was very persistent in saying no to them, and finally managed to get into the cab and lock the door. He gave Steven directions to a house in the northeastern part of the city. As they were talking, the man pulled a roll of bills out of his pocket, about three and one half inches in diameter. Steven took one look at the roll and almost crapped his pants. The man then proceeded to tell Steven that he had earned the money by writing western novels. The guy was very nice. He was really a rather quiet sort, but somehow Steven didn't believe that this fellow really was a writer. That, however, will ever remain a mystery. They arrived at the address the man had given. There was no one home, and the man asked Steven to take him back to town. On the way back, the man suggested that he take the cab on an hourly basis and they could have some fun. He put the cab on hourly. He wanted desperately to tell the "author" about himself and Herta, but there seemed to be no rush.

Finally, his passenger asked the question, "Steven, do you think we can spend this money by morning?"

"Sir, I really don't know, but we can sure as hell try!" he replied, as he almost stained his shorts again. "You mean you want to rent the cab until morning?"

"Sure, why not?"

"Say, why don't I turn the cab in, and we can use my car instead," Steven was thinking how much that 12 dollars an hour could mean to him.

The "author" replied, "That's a good idea!"

Steven let him out in front of a downtown hotel. The man paid his taxi bill, and Steven left to turn in the cab. When he returned from picking up his car, the man had disappeared. Steven never saw him again. He knew that his greediness had done him in. He would never know just how much money this fellow would have been willing to give to him.

On another occaision, he picked up a famous sports figure.

He spent several hours with him, into to the wee hours of the morning. The man's name was Tony Zale.

Herta and Steven were writing quite regularly. He received a letter every two weeks. After a very few weeks in school, Steven's German professor suggested he try to write Herta a few lines in German. Herta was not amused, and gave him the dickens. He didn't think that was quite fair.

That year, at Christmas time, Steven drove his car to Grape Arbor to spend the holidays with his mother. While he was in Grape Arbor, he and Carole went out a few times. They celebrated New Years together.

On Christmas Eve, Steven placed what was to be a very happy phone call. He called Herta and asked her to come to the United States for a visit during his summer vacation. He suggested that if they decided to get married while she was in the States, she could go home at the end of the summer to get her things and say her good-byes. There was, at this point, a very long pause, then Herta said, "Ye-yes," and then shouted for joy, "YES! YES! YES! I will come!"

He drove back, to the valley, one happy man. Describing him as happy was putting it mildly. He was in total ecstasy. He was in such a state that he could not sleep for two or three nights. When he got back to Central Valley and told his father that Herta was coming, his father was pleased and assured him that she could stay at the house. Steven knew there was a great chance this get together might fail. As far as he knew, to this point, Herta did not love him. It was still his conviction, however, that he had to know her.

Planning, between Herta and Steven, went well. He went to the bank and nervously carried six hundred dollars in cash to the travel agency. This money was enough to cover the round trip fare from Germany to New York by boat, and airfare from New York to Los Angeles.

He was in his second semester of college when, one afternoon, his stepmother came to him and told him that she wanted seventy-five dollars a month for his room and board. She also told him that she did not want him to tell his father that she asked for the money. He never told his father, but after two months he moved out because he knew that he could live cheaper on the outside. His father never did figure out why he moved out. He moved into a converted garage. He had a shower, and the room suited him fine.

Steven never had any real accidents while he was working for the cab company. The company bought cheap recap tires, however, and he found himself changing tires occasionally. On one occasion, two men ran out of the bus station, jumped into his taxi and told him that they had just missed their bus, and could he catch it for them. He agreed, and he headed his cab north. He caught the bus for them in next town. He turned the motor off and got out of the cab to collect his fare. When he returned to the cab and started his engine he found that the clutch had gone out. Here he was, twenty-five miles north of Central Valley and his cab had broke down. He had learned to shift gears without the use of a clutch. The only problem was how to start the car in neutral and get into first gear. There wasn't a way that he knew. He had but one chance, that was to put it into first gear and push on the starter. He knew if he pressed the starter the car would move forward. As the car moved, the engine caught hold, and Steven took his cab home.

Steven didn't get into much trouble at the cab company. He had only one minor accident, if you could call it that. It seems that Steven was taking some elderly ladies home one night when he ran over a curb. It bounced the cab a little, but Steven never thought a thing about it. He helped the ladies out of the cab. The next day the taxi boss invited Steven into his office and wanted to know what happened. The boss said that the women had filed a complaint, and were about to sue for damages. Well, thankfully, that was the last Steven ever heard about the incident.

Steven did manage to get a couple of tickets. Well what's a fellow to expect, driving as much as he did. Finally, one day the taxi boss called him into the office and told him that there was someone to see him in the next room. When he entered the room he found a police officer. Steven had never seen him

before, but he introduced himself as the taxi officer. He told
Steven that he had come by for a friendly chat, and if he didn't
straighten up, his ass was grass. That is, they might consider
pulling his taxi permit.

The last ticket Steven received was for driving down an
alley the wrong way at four in the morning. The police didn't
give him the ticket for his driving, but rather for the reason he
was in the alley. He was trying to find a companion for his
passenger. He didn't, and he never dealt in that trade during
the whole time he was driving cab.

This last ticket was the "straw that broke the camel's back."
He was sent a letter from the DMV inviting him to a hearing to
be held in Central Valley, just for him. He would be asked to
show cause why his license should not be revoked.

Steven was considerably upset. If he were to lose his license
he would no longer have a job. When Herta came that summer,
they would not have a way to get around. He would not be able
to get to school because it was so far away from where he lived.

The hearing was set for a Friday evening. The night before,
Steven picked up a couple who had flown down from Bay City
that afternoon. Steven had a lengthy trip with them, and as the
three of them talked along, it was decided that they would hire
him by the hour. Steven told them about Herta coming, and
about his meeting the next day with the people from the
Department of Motor Vehicles. Their names were Edward and
Jenny Smith. He owned an advertising firm in Bay City. Steven
took them to some of the better bars in town. He'd stop and go
in with them while they had a few drinks. It was a very nice
evening that could hardly be called work. At the end on the
evening, Ed gave Steven his card and said that if he ever needed
help to give him a call.

Steven reported to the Department of Motor Vehicles at
two in the afternoon. The gentlemen from Sacramento were
not particularly pleasant. They read off infractions with such
deliberateness that Steven was beginning to feel guilty, even
though he knew that two of the charges were really nonsense.

Finally, after the intense revelation. The chief license

inspector said, "Well, Mr. Mack, do you have any thing to say that might show cause why we should not suspend your driver's license?"

"Well, sir, I'm a college student, and I really need the income from driving to continue my education. There were only three violations. The first one was for going forty miles an hour in a thirty-five mile zone. It was eleven o'clock at night, and there was not another vehicle in sight, not even one parked along the road side. As far as the ticket for driving down a one way alley the wrong way, there was clearly no danger involved in this act, it was four o'clock in the morning." The police thought that Steve was looking for the entrance of a certain hotel. No such entrance was located there. Steven had never been there, before or since, Steven had never been engaged in what would be considered illegal activities.

Finally, Steven said, "My girlfriend is coming to visit me from Germany this summer. We could get by without a car, except for one problem. My girlfriend is an amputee. She wears an artificial limb above the knee. Her limited range of walking, and her fatigue rate, cut her mobility considerably. Without a car, I will not be able to show her the good time that she really deserves, and that I would like to show her."

The inspector just shook his head. "Young man, I hope that your apparent record belies itself. Please avoid any accidents. Good luck, boy, dismissed.."

Steven's underarms were completely saturated, and his face was covered with beads of sweat as he exited the DMV office. Steven thought, thank God.

Steven was working six days a week, putting in forty-eight hours a week. On the seventh evening, he was going to Army reserve meetings in order to get his full discharge early. That required two years of guard service. After several months of this, Steven arranged to skip one guard meeting. It was the first day he had actually had off since September, and now it was May. Steven went to The Grille, which was where he liked to drink. The regular bartenders, who owned the place, were not on duty that night. Steven settled down to some real beer drinking. He didn't hold his liquor well and, after three beers, he was pretty well enroute to being intoxicated. By five beers, Steven had become downright unruly. He and the bartender got into an argument over a bet they made about paying the taxi driver who would take Steven home. After the cab driver came, Steven refused to leave The Grille. The bartender became upset, and quietly summoned the police. When the police arrived, Steven could not quite understand why he was getting all this hassle since it was his first day off in a very long time. The policeman, for some reason, had but little interest in this fact. Steven raised hell all night in jail.

The judge was not pleased with that either. He asked Steven to take out all his money and lay it on the bench. Steven was carrying twenty-seven dollars. The judge carefully counted the money, instructed the bailiff to give Steven a receipt for the money, and said "That takes care of your fine, because of your rowdiness, you may go. Oh, and Mack! Try and stay out of trouble."

It was only five days until Herta was to take a train to Bramerhaven. She made one last visit to Herr Braun's to have her leg checked over for the trip. She also needed an extra role of stump pulling cloth. Herta was very excited, she had never dreamed, until two years ago, that she would ever go to the States. Now she could go for a short time and decide if she wished to live there or not.

Herr Braun greeted his favorite client with, "Well, Mein Schatz, how do you feel running off on such a long trip? How can you desert me? Who will keep you walking?"

Herta entered a booth and handed Herr Braun her leg.

"Ach, mein herr, I will return. Do you begrudge me a little recreation. I know by now that there is no one that can take care of my needs like you can."

"Well, at least, I know that he is a nice fellow. A little crazy perhaps, but a good heart," Herr Braun was saying, as he handed her back her leg.

When Herta had finished in the booth, she gave Herr Braun

a sweet kiss on the cheek. "Don't be sad, I will return. Whether we marry or not, I will be back for at least a little while."

As Herta reached the back door, of the shop, Inge showed up. She was planning to have Herr Braun check something for her, but when she saw Herta, she said, "Will you join me on the Haüpt Strässe for a cup tea?" Herta nodded yes, and Inge continued, "I'm in a bit of a hurry this morning, so let me give this to Herr Braun first. She went inside, slipped her leg off, and gave it to Herr Braun. She came out to Herta on crutches, having left her leg with the maestro.

As they approached the Haüpt Strässe, Herta walked as smoothly as she had ever walked, as Inge glided easily, even gracefully, on the crutches she borrowed from Herr Braun. Her right leg propelled her from beneath the hem of her skirt. When they reached the cafe, they each ordered tea.

Inge spoke. "You must be very excited about your trip the States, aren't you?"

"Oh, yes, of course, I have always wanted to visit the States."

"Do you love Steven, Herta?"

"You know the answer to that."

"Then why are you going?"

"Well, he is a nice fellow. You know, I have never known a man who loved me anymore than Steven. He just will not give up."

"Why don't you love him, then?"

"For one thing, he is so young and immature."

"You are only a year older than he."

"Yes, but I look for man who is mature in his profession. Steven is but a freshman in college. He doesn't dress very well either. You must admit that he isn't very handsome."

"Well, you can surely help him improve his dress. I don't think his looks are so bad. You know he is in pursuit of a higher education. He will be able to provide for you very well, someday."

"Perhaps, when I'm there, I will find that I do love him. At any rate, he has been very interested in me for the past two years. The least I can do, while I'm there, is give myself to him."

"Will such an act make Steven, as you know him, happy? He loves you, and wants you as his wife."

"Well, I'm not sure that I don't love him, I just might marry him. As we have always said, he's a good guy and there is some potential for accomplishment in him."

"When do you leave?"

"I catch the train for Bremerhaven at seven Wednesday morning."

They were finished with tea and already on the street, Inge heading for the shop on her crutches, and Herta returning to her flat, to fill another suitcase.

"I'll meet you at the train station!" cried Inge as she slipped out of sight.

It was final week at school, and Steven received a call from the telegraph office stating that Herta's plane would arrive from New York at 7:45 that evening. When Steven heard that, his heart did a flip. He was so excited that he almost missed a final that he had scheduled for that afternoon. He could hardly wait. He would finally have a chance to spend time with the one he loved.

The airport was about five miles from Steven's house. He left the house at seven o'clock. That was a whole half hour before the plane was due to arrive, but this was one time Steven did not want to be late. Steven recalled one evening a few weeks prior, when he came to the house around midnight to see his dad. He had been depressed for several days, even though he knew Herta was coming. He had only kissed her once in the two years he knew her, and that was during the week he left Germany.

Steven's dad came to the back door with a small bunch of bananas in hand. "Kind of late for you to be around, isn't it, boy?"

"Well, I let off work a little early, so that I could be here when you got home."

"You look a bit down. Nothing wrong, is there? She didn't change her mind, did she?"

"It's just that we've never even kissed and she has never said that she loves me. What if, while she's here, no romance blooms. Do you think that is possible?"

"Well, that is entirely possible, son, but do you think that any woman could accept such a trip, and then be that hard-hearted?"

"Yeah, I guess you're right. I hope that we will have a nice time together"

"Now, you run along and get your rest, and just stop worrying for once. OK?

"Yeah, I guess your right. Thanks, Dad." With that Steven raced out of the house to his car and headed for his garage room.

Steven did have a half hour wait for the plane. He went into the restaurant and had a cup of coffee as he waited. Steven, to be sure, was as nervous as a cat.

At last the announcement came over the loud speaker that flight 417 was approaching the landing strip. Steven almost jumped out of his seat as he headed out to the restraining fence to watch the plane land. It was late June, and it was hot! Herta would feel like she stepped out into an oven when she deplaned.

The plane was down now and they rolled stairs to the door of the plane. The door slid open and there stood Herta, at the exit. Steven's heart was in his throat. Herta took the rails of the stairway in her hands and walked as quickly as possible down the stairs, leading her left foot down until she reached the bottom. Then, she walked as easily as anyone else to the gate. Steven, remembering how few times he had kissed Herta, ran up to her, put his arms around her, and kissed her, before she even had a chance to see him.

She was hungry when she arrived, so she ate a turkey sandwich, while Steven had another cup of coffee. Herta was very tired from the trip. Steven claimed her luggage and they proceeded to his father's house.

When they arrived at the house, Steven's half sister, his aunt, and one of his stepsisters were there to greet them. It seemed hardly the time to be greeting people, but Herta and Steven sat down and did there best to enjoy the visit. Steven was so excited at having Herta there, he just couldn't keep his eyes off his beloved. Finally, the guests left. Dad invited Steven to stay on the couch in the front room, rather than going home that night. That was a good deal for him because he had a final early in the morning and it would be nice to be that much closer to both her, and the school. The next morning when he woke up, he was ecstatic. It must have not been much passed six. He went into the kitchen and made a pot of coffee. He took a cup to Herta where she was sleeping, which happened to be the room that used to be Steven's. Herta was sound asleep, and she wasn't about to wake for Steven or anyone else. Steven couldn't blame her, as he knew that she had been on a rough trip for the past few weeks. Steven went into the kitchen, fixed himself a cup of coffee, and studied a bit for the psychology exam he would have that morning.

That night they went to a local nightclub and watched a famed hypnotist. They wouldn't serve Herta, who was a year and a half older than Steven, a drink because they would not accept her passport as proof of age. After the show, Steven took Herta downstairs to a bar which had a large glass window behind what was a swimming pool. Steven told Herta that he knew the swimmer in the tank from school.

At the end of the night as they sat in the car in front of Steven's father's house. Steven and Herta kissed. As they did, Steven put his hand gently on her breast. She took his hand, slid it off, opened the door, said good night, and went into the house. Steven drove merrily home. She was here!

Herta and Steven were having a good time. The next day Steven, took Herta to the limb company to introduce her, so that if she had to have some work done on her leg, she would not be networking with strangers. Erich, who worked at the front desk, and Steven were friends. Frank and Arthur were the limb makers in the shop. They all went to lunch together at The Grille next door. Then Herta and Steven walked over to Main Street. He took her by a jewelry store and showed her the engagement ring he had picked out for her.

The next day, he picked her up at his dad's house at ten

o'clock. It was Saturday, and Steven had taken a two weeks vacation (without pay). Herta and he were going to the coast to visit his mother. It was hot on that desert drive between Central Valley and Grape Arbor. It did not usually get cooler until after you came down The Grade. They were having a nice time, chatting about their mutual friends in Heidelberg. Herta, told Steven all about Inge's architect job with the Army. Her little son was doing well, and Inge was happier than she had been in a very long time.

Steven and Herta were having a great time, when suddenly there was a loud noise in the area of the hood. Steven pulled over immediately, as he had no desire to injure the motor anymore than necessary. He told Herta that he thought it was a piston. Steven got out of the car to look around. The desert was hot, and flat. There appeared to be nothing around for miles. But, no, that wasn't so! Steven could see some houses slightly off to the right in the distance. They were apparently on another road, about a mile away. Steven knew that was the only way he was going to get help. He went back to the car to speak to Herta.

"Herta, there are some houses, across the desert about a mile off."

"Steven, I'm not feeling well, in this heat. I didn't want to tell you, but my period started this morning, and I'm flowing quite heavily."

"I think that's too far for you to walk, anyway, and I don't think that you would have much chance of getting very far in the sand."

"That's all right, Steven, you go ahead and go, but, please hurry."

"I'm sorry that I don't have air conditioning, but it's too late for that now."

Steven reached into the back seat and brought the canister of water into the front seat. Thankfully it was still cold. "Here, this water will help you. Whatever you do, don't drink more than a few sips at a time and don't drink very much. Water can really make you awfully sick in the heat if you don't take care."

Steven leaned over and gave Herta a kiss, she turned and

gave him a nice ripe one on his lips. With that, Steven headed across a "no man's land" toward the little clump of houses. It was hot, and a light breeze blew that seemed even hotter. The beads of sweat began to pour down his face. He took his handkerchief from his pocket and tied it around his forehead in hopes of slowing the flow of water onto his face. It helped him only a little. The only plus was that the sand on the ground was crusted, and relatively hard. Steven was able to make good time toward the settlement.

He was three quarters of the way to the houses, when he heard a sound. While it was a sound he had never heard before, it was one that he never wanted to hear. He recognized the sound, nevertheless, as that of a rattlesnake. Steven froze, and then he spotted the rattler just six feet ahead, coiled, and looking straight at him. Steven knew that he was too close for safety. It was to late now, the snake sprang. Steven back pedaled. He was only able to get back a few feet, but it was just enough to cause the snake to miss his pants leg by six inches. He turned and ran back to distance himself from the snake.

For some reason Steven forgot all about the heat, and the sweat. From that moment on he concentrated on the ground, to make sure no more snakes were able to 'sneak up' on him. By the time he reached the small, but welcomed houses, Steven was thankful to be alive. He knocked on the door of the first house. No one was home. He began to register concern thinking, what if these houses are deserted. His fears were immediately allayed as a couple, about his age, came to the door of the second house, as he knocked.

"I'm sorry to bother you folks," Steven said as the young couple came down the stairs of the house, "but my car broke down up the road, and I had to leave my girlfriend alone in it. Could you give me a hand?"

"Sure," the young man replied. "My name is Joe and my wife's name is Edna. How'd you get here?"

"My name is Steven, and I walked across this patch of desert."

"Boy, I'd never have done it, that place is full of rattle

snakes."

"Yeah, I know," replied Steven. "One darn near got me."

"Your lucky. Well, let's get the pickup around back and see what we can do."

"Good, I think it's a rod from the way it sounded." Steven said as he looked at the truck, which must have been a model from the thirties. It was a two-tone job. It was blue and rust. No, not rust color, just rust. The fenders appeared as if they were about to fall off. As a matter of fact, as Steven got a look at the truck, he found that the left one had. Steven was beginning to doubt that pickup would even make it to the car. That was until, Joe started the engine. That hood hid a monster. It must have been over three hundred horsepower, and Steven surmised that it was a V8. It damn near took Steven's head off. Quicker, than you could say "jackrabbit" they moved down the road and were at the car where Herta was patiently waiting. Steven introduced Joe to Herta. Joe told Steven, as they hooked the car up to the pickup, that there was a garage in the small town just five miles down the road from his house. They left Herta with Edna. Joe and Steven continued to the garage. Fortunately, the mechanic said that he could get on the job right away. If there were no unforeseen problems he could have the car ready by morning.

They returned to the little, cool house, and finally Steven had a chance to cool off. Edna served a wonderful meal, and as they were eating, she casually mentioned that Steven and Herta could sleep in their room that night. Steven's mouth, at least mentally, flew open a mile. He looked at Herta who had no expression at all on her face. She obviously, already knew. Steven just said, "Why, how nice of you." He didn't protest, for fear that they would change their minds.

Steven called his mother and told her what had happened, and explained to her that they would be there in the morning. After supper, they sat around the front room and talked. Joe explained that, he and Edna had come out to California from New Mexico to take a job with an exploratory oil drilling company. He said that the desert wasn't such a bad place to

live once you got used to it. It was only seventy miles either
way to Central Valley or Grape Arbor. Herta told of her life in
Germany, and Steven talked of school and taxis. It got late, and
everyone turned in.

To say that Steven was nervous and excited would be to
put it mildly. Steven went into the bathroom to change, while
Herta got ready for bed in the bedroom. Finally, Herta slipped
into the bed, and told Steven that he could come in. Steven put
out the light and slipped in beside her.

Herta rolled over toward him and gave him a little kiss and
rolled back over. It was hot in the room and Steven could not
sleep. He began to think about where he was right then. He
really couldn't believe it. Oh, he had been in bed with a woman
before, but this was the first time he had been near a woman he
loved. He knew they should not make love that evening, but
he really had no assurance that they would ever be make love.
The sleeping arrangements were made, while he and Joe were
gone to the garage. Perhaps, Herta had agreed to stay with him,
instead of having the embarrassment of admitting that they had
never been together. He was in bed with the one he loved. She
had never said that she loved him—but she was here. Steven
tried to go to sleep.

Herta suddenly moved in the bed, and Steven felt her laying
across his chest. He felt her lips press against his as he had
never felt. Her tongue passed through his teeth as she explored
the cavity of his mouth. He pressed his tongue past hers and
into her mouth. She pulled her head back, and said, "I will marry
you, Steven, I will marry you!"

They laid together arm in arm for a long time until they
were nearly asleep, in spite of the heat. Herta turned on her
side again. Steven laid on his back thinking, I don't give a damn
if I don't sleep!

The next morning they were once again treated to a
scrumptious meal. Herta and Steven were beside themselves
with joy and excitement. Joe and Edna must have assumed
that it had been a much more active night than it was.

The garage called to inform them that the car was ready

and Joe took Steven and Herta to their car. From then on, thankfully, it was an uneventful trip. As they continued, the weather grew hotter, until they got on the downward side of The Grade. Then the temperature began to fall to a more reasonable level. Perhaps it was the sea breeze that reached the small valley in which Grape Arbor was situated or perhaps not, but Grape Arbor was blessed with a year-round average temperature of seventy-two degrees.

Steven took Herta to his cousin's house where his mother was now living. It was a fairly new track nestled between two mountains. Steven and Herta had a wonderful two week vacation. After being there for several days, Steven's cousin, Herta, and he went the beach. Steven loved the beach. It was a most beautiful beach. It had a reasonable surf, with waves that were never particularly vicious. He had learned to swim, or more correctly, play in the ocean, at this beach, when he was a teenager. Now he was back to enjoy it once again. Herta, who was wearing an off the shoulder top, sat on a blanket against the beach wall and soaked in the sun while Steven swam.

Finally, when Steven came back to Herta, to rest, she suggested they go for a walk. They walked over to the pier, and as they got there Herta stopped, put her arm around him and gave him a big kiss, as she whispered in his ear.

"Tonight?" he asked, with a big grin.

"Yes," the reply came with all definiteness.

Around the dinner table that night there was a sense of excitement. It would seem that everyone at the table knew what was happening, except for the three little children. It was the first time in his life that Steven didn't care if he ate or not. He tried to eat in a polite, speedy manner. Herta had a grin on her face that could not have been wiped off with a hot towel.

Finally, dinner was over, and Herta helped Steven's cousin with the dishes. That being over, she went into her room and got her purse. She was dressed in a red skirt with a black blouse. Steven said that they were going out for a little while, and that they would be back in a couple of hours. They got into the car, and drove toward the beach. Steven took a street that led directly to the beach front. Just at the end of the road there was a sand dune, perhaps fifteen feet high, just off to their right. He pulled over to the left hand edge of the road. It was nearing sunset, and they remained in the car and watched the beautiful sunset that turned the beach to near darkness.

Steven got out of the car, and went around to help Herta out. He opened the trunk of the car and got out a pillow and blanket, which his father had given him. It was quite a steep climb up the dune, but Steven took Herta by the arm and they made it up quite easily. Steven spread the blanket on the sand, and they both sat. The bright full moon made the white sand glisten around their blanket. They laid back on the blanket and could feel the soft sand under them. They were gazing at the moon and saying nothing. They were savoring the moment.

Steven turned toward Herta, and for the first time, touched a button on her blouse. As he did, her left hand slid his away. As she came to a sitting position, she took hold of the bottom part of her blouse, one part in each hand, and pulled it opened, revealing her beautiful white breasts in the moonlight. Steven was more than a little shocked because he had no idea that she was not wearing a bra. Steven sat up and started to undress. Herta slipped the blouse off her shoulders, and put it on the blanket beside her. He watched her as she continued to remove her clothes. She remove the wide black belt from around her waist. She pulled the hem of her skirt out from under her, revealing her half-slip, and placed it by her blouse. She removed her half-slip in the same manner. She slipped her shoe off her right foot. She unhooked her garter belt from her right stocking and slipped the stocking off and placed it in her shoe. She released the garter belt from her left stocking, and pulled it out from under her underpants. Now she placed both open palms, one on each side of her leg and slid her stocking along the wooden thigh until it was beyond her knee. This revealed a strap, which was hooked near the lip of the leg. As she unhooked the strap, the knee cover flipped down over the knee. She then reached down along the outside of her leg, and unscrewed a valve, which was about the size of a fifty cent piece. She then placed the heels of her hands, one on each side, on the lip of her leg and pushed. Her left leg slipped off her thigh. Her stump lie bare on the blanket.

What had cause Herta to lose her leg was ugly, but Herta was in no way any less than beautiful. As she slipped her panties over her stump, and off her foot, Steven knew that he had chosen the right person. All he wanted was her love.

They lay back on the blanket, with nothing to come between them. They looked at each other almost with wonder, turned toward each other, and held each other tenderly. Steven put his hand between her thighs and she massaged his penis. She took the pillow and put it under her buttocks. Steven slipped his thighs gently between hers. They brought each other joy.

After what seemed many hours of an impossible dream, Steven stood up, and offered her his hand. She took it and stood with him. As Steven steadied her on her foot, they held each other very close as they embraced in the moonlight. The light played bright highlights on her coal black hair. Her white skin became almost unreal in its whiteness. The inside of her left thigh rested lightly on the outside of Steven's right thigh. Steven watched, as Herta put her leg on.

She took a long piece of thin woolen tubular cloth and pulled it up over her stump, then she dropped the long end of the cloth into the wooden shaft of her prosthesis. She pulled the cloth through the round opening from which she had pulled the plug earlier, and pressing down with her body into the opening, pulled the cloth through, pulling the end of her leg snugly into the socket. She then screwed the valve back into the shaft of her leg, and pushing on the center of the valve, released a little more air, allowing for better suction.

They returned to the car, and stopped at a small cafe, for a cup of coffee. As they sat across from each other in the cafe, Steven was still not conscious of the fact the Herta was not wearing a bra. As he looked at her, his heart was filled with love for her and he realized that the piece was no longer missing, for Herta had given it back, and he was ecstatic. He had found his love and, at last, he could experience full joy. Thank God for

Herta. Steven was at last a very happy man.

The next afternoon, they went downtown and rented a pair of crutches, from a wheelchair rental shop. They knew that, with all good luck with the car, they would return to Central Valley the next day.

That evening they decide to eat out, for their last night on the coast. They picked a rather nice restaurant, not far from the beach. After they had a delicious steak dinner, they drove down the coast and found a deserted strip of beach. Steven was able to pull the car to within fifteen yards of the shore line where the water lapped lazily at the sand. It was already dark, and the full moon of the previous evening still smiled on them. Steven removed his clothes, to reveal a bathing suit under them. Herta removed her leg and her shoe. She took the crutches and headed over the sand toward the water. Steven followed her at a distance. Each step with the crutches flipped a little sand. There was a gentle breeze, and the wind, which blew warmly on their faces, blew the right side of her skirt so that it surrounded her leg, and then uncurled. Steven, at this moment, was very glad that he, and no one else, was with Herta. He felt lucky.

As Steven caught up with her, she said, "The sand feels different from anything I have ever felt. It is soft, but firm, and it is warm. Its firmness sustains my foot well.

As she reached the water's edge. Steven walked a little further out than Herta so that he could walk alongside of her. Her crutch tips sank but an inch into the wet sand, and as the water from the tide washed over her foot, she said, "It feels as if the sand on which I'm standing might be washed away."

After they had played along the surf for about an hour, they returned to the car. Herta stood up close to Steven, laying her stump on his thigh as she whispered in Steven's ear, "Steven, can you find a place where we are alone?"

Steven looked around a little and said, "We're alone no— Oh! Yes! I think I can."

He reached into the back of the car to get the pillow and blanket, and they headed for the nearest sand dune.

The next day, they headed for Central Valley. On the way

home, they stopped to visit the friends who were so much help in getting the car fixed on the trip over. They enjoyed some refreshments and the headed for home. It was quite late when they arrived in Central Valley, so they stayed at Steven's place.

In the morning, Steven took Herta to his dad's place and they told him that they were going to get married. Then Steven went to work. The next day, Herta and Steven got their marriage license. After talking with Steven's mother, they decided to get married in two weeks. They stopped by the jeweler's and Steven bought the ring he had shown to Herta earlier. Herta put it on immediately.

On Thursday, after checking in his cab, Steven decided to call Herta before he went home. His stepmother answered the phone and told him that Herta was not home. She did not have any idea where she was. Steven went to The Grille to see if she was there. She was not, and neither were any of their friends from next door. Steven ordered a beer. No one in the bar knew where any of them were. Steven became upset. He had no idea where she was. The upset that he felt was not all from this incident, but also came from experiences of his earlier life, which seemed emotionally indistinguishable to him.

Steven continued to drink and call home. He became fearful that she was with another man, and all hell broke loose in him. He was pretty drunk by then. He knew where one of the fellows lived, across the street from the bar. He almost knocked the door down before he gave up and realized that there was no one there.

By the time he returned to the bar, his father was there to take him home. They did not speak a word. They just looked at each other. It was as if they had spoken a book to each other. His dad put his arm around Steven and walked him to his car. The drive home was silent. When they arrived home, Herta was there. She did not realize at first the gravity of this matter for Steven. When Steven finally explained it to Herta, she apologized to him. She assured him that this wouldn't happen again. Steven was still a bit apprehensive, and still very drunk at bedtime. Herta took him to bed with her. It was by far the safest thing to do.

Dad took all of the alcohol in the house with him, into his bedroom. In Steven's condition he couldn't be trusted. Steven was too drunk to want anything more than to go to sleep. Herta made over him, and tried to make up to him for what she had done. It was no use, right then. Steven was out like a light.

The next morning, before they were barely awake, a hand came through the door, motioning for Steven to get out of Herta's bedroom. It was Steven's stepmother and she was a bit angry. Steven did so post haste.

The day before the wedding, while at work, Steven began to have some concerns about the marriage. Ordinarily, that seems to be a normal thing on the day before a wedding, but it got out of hand. That afternoon, while working, he received a call from his mother, who had just arrived from Grape Arbor for the wedding. He left work and went to meet her. They met at one of the more popular bars in town, and decided to have a drink. Steven thought that this was a good idea, because he thought he might forget his problem. When they were seated, they started to talk, and Steven started telling his mother about his misgivings. His mother tended to agree with him. The more they talked and drank, the more upset Steven became.

Finally, his mother decided that he had had enough, and so they went to the little garage, made over into a house, which Steven and Herta had rented. When they got there, Herta was not there. Steven called his Dad's house, and found that she was there. Steven sent a cab for her.

When Herta arrived at the house, Steven was completely out of hand. There was no excuse for the way he acted toward Herta. He brought up all the things he thought she had done wrong. He told her that he wasn't going to marry her. By the time he was finished, she was in tears. His mother was now on Herta's side. It was one hell of a mess. Finally, Steven passed out, and when he woke up Herta was able to reason with him. She wanted to marry him.

There was no question in Steven's mind about loving Herta. He had loved her, almost, from the first moment they had met.

It was Steven's obsession with the idea that she might not really care for him and love him that was the problem. To this point, he had not heard her say that she loved him. He hoped that all would go well, and to that end, he apologized for his behavior.

The marriage ceremony was to be held in the house of the judge. Steven's old dancing partner from high school, Teddy, and his wife were the best man and matron of honor. Steven's dad and stepmother were there. Steven's half-sister was also there. Steven's mother did not attend the ceremony. After the way Steven had acted, she decided not to go, and returned to Grape Arbor. After the ceremony, there was a small reception in the backyard of Steven's dad's place.

Steven and Herta spent three days in Yosemite on their honeymoon, a wedding gift from Steven's mother. They saw a most beautiful rendition of the fire falls at Camp Curry. It was complete with calls, up an down, ending with "LET THE FIRE FALL."

They returned to their little garage, and things began to get sticky again. For some reason, Herta wanted to go to the mountains every weekend. Steven was not much of a mountain man, but because he thought the mountains must remind Herta of home, he took her. Then Herta started inviting one of the limb makers from the shop to go along. Steven could not understand why she had to have another man around on one of the very few days that he was able to spend with her. Steven was also concerned because she was leaving, with no certain return date.

It proved to be an enjoyable two months that they had together. One problem was that Steven was going broke fast. About this time they found out from the limb company that a new rubber cover had been developed for artificial limbs that, under nylons, looked perfect. It was easily installed, slipping right over the existing leg cover, without requiring any alterations. It was priced at fifty dollars, which was not all that cheap in those days. Steven was thinking about the cover, and how great it would be for Herta. She already had an almost unheard of perfect walk. Steven came home one day after work, thinking that he would suggest that they get the cover for her. When he arrived, he was greeted with a plea that they get the cover for her before she returned to Germany. Steven agreed, and an appointment was made to go to Bay City to get the cover.

Steven took the day off and they drove to Bay City early in the morning. They arrived at the prosthetic product company right on time. As soon as they arrived, Herta went into a dressing room and removed her leg. In less than an hour, they had put the new cover on and gave it the proper color to match her flesh leg. When she had put her leg back on, a local limb maker came into the store as they were leaving. The man who provided the cover, called the limb maker's attention to Herta. He watched her walk, and it took him quite a while to discover which of Herta's legs was artificial. This was a high compliment to Herta's dedication and walking skill.

That afternoon they visited with Edward and Jenny Smith at their advertising firm. The Smith's were such wonderful people and Steven and Herta had a very nice time visiting with them. Edward took quite a lot of time telling Steven about the mobile advertising units he installed in grocery stores. The units were sponsored by a large brewery. The Smiths apologized for not being able to take them out for dinner that evening, but they had a prior commitment they had to keep.

Steven and Herta went to China Town for dinner. Afterward, they started for home, reminiscing about the nice day they had and how, all to soon, they would be parting for a while. They were nearing home, when all of a sudden, they heard a sound that was all to familiar to them by now. The sound was coming from the engine, and sure enough it was another rod gone out. Steven pulled the car off the road and into a field, so as to prevent too much damage. It was the middle of the night, and the nearest person that they knew lived in Central Valley. There was nothing to be done but for both of them to get out on the road and hitchhike.

When they got to the highway, the very first vehicle to come by was a big diesel. Thank the Lord, it stopped. Fortunately Herta found little trouble getting into the truck, with a some help from Steven. When they arrived in Central Valley, Steven called a cab, to take them home. It was nearing the time when Herta would be going home. She was feeling all right about it, but Steven was already showing signs of stress over it.

Steven's mother called and talked them into letting her come over and drive them to Southland to catch the plane. Herta packed up, and they went to 'The Grille', one last time, so she could say good-bye to their friends. When Steven's mother arrived on that Friday night, Herta was ready to leave. They went over to say good-bye to Steven's dad and stepmother.

The trip to Los Angels was uneventful. They stayed at Steven's cousin's in the valley. His mother lent them her car, and Steven and Herta had fun touring the city and taking in the sites. Steven asked Herta to send him a telegram before she boarded the ship. She promised to do it.

The morning that Herta was to leave, Steven's mother drove them to the airport. Steven was allowed to board the plane to help Herta get settled. When they were ready to board the regular passengers, Steven put his arms around Herta, and gave her a big kiss. He was unable to keep the tears back any longer, and he started to cry. Herta looked him in the eye, signaling to him that he needn't cry and everything was going to turn out fine. As Steven finally left the plane, and returned to the ground, he turned and looked at the offensive plane, and thought, I'll never see her, again!

Suddenly, a pang of fear swept over Steven, as he realized how dangerously near he was to losing the piece again. Perhaps, he never really had it back. Did she really marry him in sincerity, or did she have, perhaps, another priority? Perhaps she did it for the ring. He might never know. He knew that he loved her very much, and wanted to settle down for life with her. Would she come back? He had no way of being sure. He could only wait and hope, and see if she would really give him back the piece . . .

The next day, Steven got the telegram from Herta. It asked him for thirty-five dollars to get another berth on the boat so that she would not have to walk up and down so many dangerous stairs. Steven sent her the money. It was the last thirty-five dollars he had to his name.

Steven returned home and tried to work. He had a very difficult time concentrating on anything. He missed Herta, and he worried about getting the money to bring her back. He registered for school. On the first day of school, he went to talk to a financial counselor. The counselor told him that, based on his work record and school record, the school would be happy to lend him the money he needed. Steven had a streak of pride, or something, because he decided he couldn't accept such a loan, even though there was no time constraint or interest connected to it.

When Steven got home that day, he called Edward in Bay City and told him that he was going to leave school, in order to earn enough money to bring Herta back to America. Edward told him to come on over to Bay City and work for him. He offered Steven a starting salary of ninety dollars a week.

Steven told his father about what he felt he must do. His dad seemed upset about the situation. As a matter of fact, he told Steven that if he went to Bay City, he should never return to Central Valley. That upset Steven. He did not understand why his father said this for many years. It was really not as heavy as it sounded. His father was venting some never expressed frustration.

Steven bought a metal trunk to put his possessions in, bought a bus ticket, and went to Bay City, leaving his prized car behind.

On the trip, Steven was a very sad person, indeed. He was becoming depressed. He was leaving his school behind, because he needed his wife even more than he need it. He had no time table for her return, indeed one had not yet been discussed. The only hope that Steven had was in the job that Edward had offered him. There was no way to happiness for Steven until Herta returned.

When Steven arrived in Bay City, he hauled his metal trunk onto a streetcar and watched out for a hotel. He spotted one just off Main Street. After having taken the room by the week, he settled down to write Herta a love note. He was happy about writing it, and was looking forward to receiving an answer from Herta. If for no other reason, he wanted to see it signed with love. It would be the first time he had ever received a letter from her signed with love.

It was Sunday evening, and Steven went to eat and turned in early. Monday would be his first day of work for Edward.

On Monday morning, he dressed and headed for Edward's shop. It was but a short walk from his hotel. That is why he had picked this particular hotel. Perhaps Steven felt a little better than he had been feeling. There seemed to be a glimmer of hope in this job. However, Steven could never feel really good about anything without his Herta. He walked along hurriedly. Soon he was walking a back street in Bay City where the jitney taxis ran. As he passed under the streetcar tracks, he soon came to Edward's shop. There was a freight elevator flush to the street. Steven entered and went up one floor to where Edward did business and stored his advertising materials.

As soon as Steven arrived, Edward told him that they were going to install one of the advertisements for beer in a nearby market that morning. He told Steven that it would give him a very good idea of what he would be doing. They took the equipment they would need and put it in the pickup. They drove to the market where they would put up the display. The installation portrayed the head of a man in the front of what looked like a helicopter. It was on a long pole, and Edward and Steven stacked six packs of the advertised beer around the pole. Steven watched as Edward went up the pole and put the helicopter in place. After the installation they went to a nearby pub to have a beer and eat lunch. They worked together like this for over a week, with Edward always going up the ladder to install the helicopter. Things were going on fine, except that Steven was obviously nervous. He was sure that Edward was aware of it. He knew that it had to do with Herta. He could not help it, he was worried about her. If he were to be honest with himself, he did not have total confidence that she would ever return. He was in a hell of a fix.

After a week and a half, while they were out installing a

mobile, Edward asked Steven if he would like to try putting up the helicopter. Steven said he would. He took the mobile in his hands and started up the ladder. He was about half way up, when he looked down. He started to shake and became unsteady. He tried to move up. Instead he froze. He could not move. He looked for Edward, who was busy momentarily with another matter. In fear, he looked down and as his gaze went again toward the floor he became disoriented. The floor seemed to be turning, first slowly, and then faster. The whole store seemed to close in on him. He didn't want to drop the mobile, but he knew that he was going to fall. As Steven started to leave the ladder, the mobile in hand, Edward saw what was happening. He started to run toward the ladder, but it was too late. Steven came crashing down, his face on the bubble in which the little pilot sat. The bubble smashed against the floor, with Steven's face on it. Edward rushed over and picked Steven up off the floor. Steven was not so much hurt as shaken by the fact that he had fallen. Steven was almost in tears.

Edward tried to comfort him as he checked him over for injuries. There was but one small cut from the bubble near Steven's eye. The store manager showed up, almost immediately, with a first aid kit to patch up the small wound. Steven just sat on the floor for a few minutes. Right at this time, he was not sure whether or not he would be able to stand up. Finally, after a while he was able to.

Edward talked to the store manager and apologized to him for what happened. He told him, that he would install another mobile the next day. Edward put his arm on Steven's shoulder to give him a little reassurance as they walked out to the truck together.

They got into the truck, and Edward drove to a little tavern, which was a favorite of his for lunch. When they got inside, and were seated, Edward started a very serious conversation with Steven.

"Steven, I'm not going to be able to use you for installations. I'm sorry, you're not the tough, unbeatable kid I thought you were when we first met in Central Valley. You are much more upset over Herta than I had imagined possible. Right now, I can't use you for installations. Do you understand?"

"Yes, I understand, and I am truly sorry for what happened." Steven's head was bowed, and he was on the verge of tears.

"If you like, you can still work for me. I'll have you work around the shop. I would have to cut your salary to seventy-five dollars a week, but there is a chance that you could go back on installation, once you've calmed down a bit."

"I'd like to think it over, can I come over in the morning and talk to you about it?"

"Sure, that will be fine," Edward replied.

Steven left the shop, and moved slowly toward his hotel. Just before he rounded the corner to his hotel he saw a lady and young girl just ahead of him. She was wearing what Steven took to be a brownie uniform. It had a short skirt. The girl couldn't have been more than twelve years old. She was walking on crutches, and her left leg was missing above the hem of her skirt. Steven was distressed. He was overcome with compassion. It was so hard to just stand there and look at her. He wanted so much to do something for her. He wanted to help in some way, but he knew there was nothing that he could do. Steven was almost weeping with his agony. He asked God why such a thing had to happen to such a lovely young girl. Steven went to his hotel, laid on his bed, and wept.

He got up late the next morning. The hotel clerk handed him a letter as he went by the desk. His heart did a flip. He had finally received the letter he had most anxiously awaited from his Herta. He raced up to his room, turned on the light, sat at the dresser, and tore the letter open.

Liber Steven,

I don't understand why you quit school. How will we be able to have a good life socially or financially if you do not finish school. I think that you must stay in school. You must not be thinking very well to do such a thing.

The money for the upgrade of the passage on the boat

was much appreciated.

The trip home was a nightmare. The Atlantic was terribly rough, and I was sick most of the trip. The sea was so rough that I was afraid to try to walk, so I spent much of the trip in my bunk. I am just now beginning to feel like a normal human being. I hope for the best for you Steven. I do not know when we will see each other again.

Yours,
Herta

Steven's eyes burned, as he stared at the letter in utter disbelief. His new bride had signed the letter with yours, and not with love as Steven had known full well she would. The tears streamed down Steven's face. He could feel them running hot on his cheeks. He was stunned, as if he had been hit with a sledge hammer. Just one missing word was enough for Steven. He was looking for needed encouragement from Herta. Instead, the missing word plunged into him like a knife. He had never in his life suffered such a cruel blow. After all, what would it have cost her sign the letter with love, and perhaps encourage him on the venture he had undertaken for the both of them? As the tears fell, Steven felt ill. If he felt a bit depressed over his job yesterday, he felt even more depressed over this letter.

Steven found that, increasingly since Herta left, he was spending more and more time on the street, and in crowds. He was pretty well convinced that Herta would never come back. He now found himself watching everywhere he went with an intenseness that strained his eyes. At times his eyes darted about as he moved or drove from place to place. At other times he appeared to be staring. His eyes had a very unhealthy look about them. Steven had become a man who was obviously very ill at ease. The piece was once again missing. That meant work. Finding an amputee who was satisfactory to both parties was a monumental task.

Steven would go anywhere he thought he might find a one legged lady. Sometimes he walked through hospitals, and sometimes he hung around near limb companies. It was seldom that ventures proved fruitful. He, nevertheless, believed that without looking he would be without anyone. He was not ready for that.

Since meeting Cynthia, Steven believed that he could not be happy with a physically whole person. Steven was really looking for a woman with the power of living that Cynthia possessed. Unfortunately, it took Steven a very long time to understand that her power did not lie in her disability. He could not understand that she would have been a fantastic person even if she were whole. Steven had not the smallest conception of how powerful the woman would become in the future. That still left Steven with the problem of how to look for that woman. Steven had to find the piece. Herta had faked him.

When Steven had finished crying he took off his clothes and took another shower. It was the warmth of the shower that finally soothed him to a point that he felt that he could go out to see his boss. After he dressed, he walked as briskly as he could in the hope he would be straightened up before he reached Edward's shop. Steven told Edward about the letter. Edward was not pleased by the letter, and he wished he could do something to really help Steven, but he really couldn't at the time.

Edward and Steven talked for a while, with Edward offering Steven the position in the warehouse. Steven had the feeling that he should take the job, but his foolish pride got in his way. Edward took Steven out to lunch and they talked for a long time. Edward did all he could to encourage Steven, but at this point, nothing seemed to make things any better for Steven.

Finally, Steven told Edward that he could not accept the new position. He had to move and try to find a place where he could get Herta back as quickly as possible. Edward was indeed sorry that Steven felt that way, but he understood his feelings.

The next morning Steven picked up the classified ads in the *Bay City Chronicle* and started looking through them. He spotted a job as a sandwich man in a restaurant, in a little station directly across from where Edward had his shop. He worked in the place for two weeks before he was fired.

He picked up his final check and headed for the hotel. As he neared the hotel, he saw the headline in the newspaper announcing the first orbiting satellite put into space by the Russians, known as Sputnik. It was another reason for Steven to be depressed. The thought that the Russians had accomplished something ahead of the Americans shot unrealistic fear through the hearts of many Americans. Steven already had plenty to be upset about, without this.

When he got to the hotel, he called his mother in Grape Arbor, in the course of the conversation, he told her about all what had happened since he left Central Valley, including the distressing letter from Herta. He told her about losing his two jobs. He told his mother that he was at his wit's end, and that he did not know how he would ever get Herta back to the States. His mother knew how distraught and depressed he was. She knew that he was really in need of help.

She said, "Come home, baby!" It just slipped out of her. She really didn't mean it, like it sounded. The moment she said it, she said, "I'm sorry, son, I really didn't mean it that way. You come to Grape Arbor and stay with me, while we get you some help."

Steven packed his trunk and carried it to the bus station. He was glad to get out of Bay City, but now his future looked very uncertain, and he was heavily depressed. To Steven, at this point, there was no way out. All he could see before him was bleakness. The piece was now missing for certain, and there was no way to regain it. He had lost it before he even had a chance to really enjoy it. He had no money. He was going to live now with his mother. He had no connections in Grape Arbor. Not only was the piece gone, but now he was so far down into depression he felt as though he were dead. There was nothing for him. He grieved over Herta until his whole body ached.

As he road the bus toward Grape Arbor, his mind focused on the only dog he had ever owned. He had gotten it from his mother and father as a surprise when he was about eight years old, through the city dog catcher. Steven loved his dog, which already had the name Rusty. He was a cocker spaniel. Steven took him for long walks on the circus grounds, which were very near to where he lived. Steven was quite responsible for his dog. He fed him and groomed him regularly. After he had had the dog for a couple of months, Rusty disappeared one day. Steven was heart broken over the loss and was so saddened that he moped around for weeks. He was member of the Cub Scouts, and attended meetings every Wednesday after school. One afternoon during the middle of the scout meeting, which was held indoors, Rusty came bouncing into the front room and Steven saw him. Steven could not contain himself, and demanded to know what his dog was doing in this house. They tried to explain that the dog had belonged to them before they had decided to give it up. Now that Rusty had returned on his own home, they wanted to keep him. Steven left crying and enraged. It was a terribly painful experience. It happened within a block of where he was burned several years later.

The bus down shifted. It was beginning its slow descent down The Grade. For Steven it was to be like a descent into hell. His very dignity was forfeit. He did not realize it at the time. What he did know was that he had lost everything he had just a year ago. There was now nothing but bleakness. Steven's mother met him at the bus station, and they drove to his cousin's house. His mother was still living there. They stayed the night, but Steven's mother told him that they would have to move because his cousin was fearful of his "mental problems." Steven's mother found a house, within a day or two, and they moved.

The offer for psychological help was really empty. There was no help available in Grape Arbor at that time, and there was no money to send Steven to a therapist in another town. There was nothing. Steven laid around for about a month, and fretted. He did as he pleased. He mostly wandered around town, or watched television. He felt as if he were more dead than alive. He was at a total loss as to what he was to do.

Finally, he took a job as a door to door salesman selling patent medicines and cooking extracts. He earned about ten dollars a day. The job got old fast.

He went to see a doctor he had know since he was a child. He told him about Herta in Germany, and how crushed he was because she seemed so completely lost to him. The doctor took Herta's address from him and wrote to her, pleading his case. Two weeks later, Steven got a letter from Herta, telling him that she wanted the doctor to keep his nose out of their business. More distress for Steven.

Finally, one day, he got up and went out to Arbor State College to see about registering for school. He thought he might like to be a high school drama teacher. He talked to Dr. James, who was acting head of the English Department. Dr. James indicated to Steven that he could become a drama teacher by studying in the English Department. Steven didn't look twice, he just decided that this was something he would like to do. It was something that he could do. Steven registered and started school within a week. His classes were mostly English classes. During the year and a quarter that he was at Arbor State, he did not find much satisfaction in his studies. He never did take any drama classes. There almost were none. The goal of the department was to train English teachers. That was all right with Steven, but drama was his interest. He did not do well in his studies while he was at Arbor State. He felt that he had been misled by Dr. James when he talked him into entering Arbor State. However he decided to see it through and get his teaching credentials.

Actually, during this short time that Steven was at Arbor State, English was not his major, but rather chess. Steven was not a great chess player. He liked to play at lunch. He joined the chess club, and eventually became president of the club. This was the one bright spot for Steven while he was at Arbor State. After Steven became president of the club, Dr. James, who was also the chess club advisor, suggested to Steven that the Arbor State Chess Club should sponsor the California Intercollegiate Chess Championships. Steven took the task to heart and managed to produce the tournament. He contacted all of the universities, colleges, and junior colleges in the state. He arranged with the merchants in town to donate money for trophies and other prizes. He arranged for a victory banquet to be held in the Greyhound bus station restaurant. The manager of the restaurant was a friend of Steven's and gave the group a great meal, including steak, at a very reasonable price. There were about twenty-five players from around the state for the two day event. Everyone seemed to have a wonderful time.

Steven was beginning to get a bit desperate in his life alone. Occasionally, when he was very drunk, he would call Cynthia on the phone. Sometimes her husband would answer, but he always let her talk. Cynthia was always sympathetic, and tried to soothe him. He was always too drunk to get what he probably should have from the talks, but it felt good to talk to her again.

A few friends of Steven's and he stayed up one night until long after midnight. They were not college students. They decided in the wee hours of the morning to take off for Southland. When they got to Southland, they told him that they would meet him in Nearlake later in the afternoon. The first thing Steven did was go to the newspaper office and place a personal ad in the paper stating that he wanted to meet a girl about his age, and that his previous wife was an amputee.

Having done that, Steven took a stroll around town. As he was walking along the street, he saw a women ahead of him limping. She was dressed in an old pair of jeans and an old shirt. She had a heavy load of books in her arms, and was obviously headed for the library. She stopped to look at a picture in the window of the building they were in front of.

"Isn't that an unusual picture of Winston Churchill?" Steven asked.

"Why, yes," she replied, "I never thought that I would see him looking like that."

"Are you going to the library?" he asked.

She looked at him in disbelief as she shifted the weight of the books. "Why, as a matter of fact, I am. How perceptive of you."

"Might I carry some of those books for you?" he asked, as he reached and took the majority of the load from her and continued, "My name is Steven Mack, what's yours?"

She replied, "My name is Anne Wells. Are you going to the library?"

"I've got all of your books, so I guess I'd better, don't you think?"

"Oh, you really don't have to do this on my account."

"It's my pleasure. After we're finished at the library, would you have a drink with me?"

"Oh, I'm afraid that I don't drink."

"Would you join me for lunch?"

"Yes, I might consider that."

They delivered the books and Steven waited while Anne selected a couple of books to take home. Then they went to a nearby restaurant and started talking. She told him about the job she had downtown, and about her interest in art. He told her about going to school and being in Germany. She finally mentioned that she had lost her leg below the knee and was wearing a prosthesis. She never, ever said how it happened. After lunch, they wandered around town together, and she took him into a dress shop with her and tried on a couple of poor, inexpensive dresses. It was approaching the time when Steven would have to head for Nearlake. He invited Anne to join him and his friends for a trip to the amusement pier that evening. She thought about it, but decided to pass it up. She did, however give Steven her work address, and asked him to stop by the next time he came to town.

The gang went to the amusement park and had a very nice time. Steven found the trip home rather enjoyable. At last he had found a girl that he might enjoy being near. He was back to school only a few days, when he received an answer to his advertisement. It was from a girl by the name of Barbara Chein, in Orange county. She had lost her leg to cancer two years before, and had just moved to California. She gave him the address of the hotel she was staying at, and said that she would like very much to meet him. Steven wrote back and they started corresponding. At this particular time, it was late summer, and Steven didn't have the money to visit Barbara. A couple of months later, Steven tried to call her, but she had moved.

Around Christmas time, Steven had rounded up enough cash to take another trip to Southland. Steven arrived in Southland on Sunday night. The next morning, he went to the business establishment where Anne worked. He inquired about her at their personnel office. After several minutes of waiting, Anne appeared at the door of the office with a broad smile. She was delighted to see him, as was he to see her.

After they had talked for a few minutes, Anne said, "Steven, why don't you come back for lunch, and I'll have you as my guest."

"Gee! That sounds great," Steven said, and after a few minutes he left.

At noon, Steven was standing in front of the fifth floor elevator doors, as Anne had told him to do. The elevator door popped open, and Anne came out. She took Steven's hand, and ushered him into the cafeteria. They had a delightful lunch together. They agreed to meet after work and go to dinner. The conversation over lunch was light. They really had a good time together. Anne told Steven that she worked in the mail room. She had been with the company for ten years.

That evening they had dinner at a small sidewalk cafe in the center of Southland. Steven told Anne about being an English major at Arbor State. He told her that he wanted to be a drama teacher, but the possibilities of that did not look to promising. Anne told him that she was tired of her job, but didn't really know what she could do about it. All she knew was working in that mail room.

When dinner was over, Anne invited Steven to her house. They caught the bus. They got off and walked a short block to her house. Anne got her keys out and indicated a small house at the back of the court. Steven took the key and opened the door. He reached for the light as they entered, but discovered that it was on the other wall. Anne turned it on and went to the bedroom and dropped her bag. Steven asked Anne for a drink of water, and Anne offered him a Coke instead. When Anne returned with the Coke, Steve slipped his arms around her waist and they kissed.

Anne pointed to the couch, and as she did, she turned the television on. It was a portable, and as she turned it on she rolled it right in front of them on the couch. They sat close together as they watched the tube, holding hands. Steven put his arm around her shoulder and they embraced. At the same time, he put his other hand on her skirt. As he pulled his hand back, her skirt came above her knees. Anne looked over at Steven and smiled. She reached over and pulled her skirt down over the left knee. That was her good leg. Her stump sock was showing above her leg through her nylon.

He put his hand on her knee. There was a strap attached to her prosthesis on either side and held on by a hook which attached to a belt buckled around her waist. Steven tried to unhook the belt through Anne's nylon. Not having much success, he slid his hand along the top of her leg and undid her garter on the top of her nylon. Anne looked over at him with a little smile, and slid her hand up the underside of her leg and undid the other garter strap. She rolled her stocking down and tied it off on her prosthesis. She then reached down into her skirt and released the belt. Steven reached over and slid the hook out of the strap. Anne pulled the strap out of her skirt. She was glad to be rid of it. She folded it and put it on the couch. Steven gave Anne a gentle kiss. Anne reached under her knee and unbuckled the strap which held her leg on. She slipped the strap forward off her knee.

After a few moments, she lifted her leg. Her stump came out of the leg. Steven picked up the leg and set it aside. Anne laid her knee over Steven's. With nothing more being done by either of them, the white stump sock fell to the floor as they watched television. Steven picked up the sock and slid it onto the top of the leg. He was just a bit excited by now at seeing her stump.

He got up and got himself a drink of water. Anne bent her knee and put it under her skirt. When he returned Anne lifted her stump out from under her skirt. She offered him her hands and he helped her stand. He stepped up against her body and they embraced for a long while. She balanced easily on her left foot. Then they sat back down.

Anne remarked, "I feel like a pelican when I stand without my leg.

Anne once again put her stump over Steven's knee. Steven reached down and cupped his palm over the end. He very gently massaged it, to Anne's obvious delight.

Anne whispered, "That feels so good, Steven. Please, don't stop."

"Don't worry, I won't." Steven replied, "I have never done this with anyone before. My wife never allowed my hand near hers. I didn't try very hard with her. It is so nice to touch you this way, it does feel good."

They enjoyed that evening together. They turned the television off and talked. About midnight, Steven decided he had better go home if he was going to catch a bus. Anne agreed because she had to go to work in the morning. Anne stood, and Steven gave her a loving kiss. She hopped over to the door, and let him out.

The next morning, Steven went to Anne's office. They told him that she had called in sick. Steven caught a bus, and went out to the house. Anne met him at the door dressed in blue denim jeans, a white blouse, and a pair of crutches. Her right pants leg was empty.

Steven, on seeing this, asked, "Are you all right, did you hurt yourself? They told me at the office, that you called in sick."

Anne shook her head, "No! No! I'm just fine, perhaps a little shaken, by last night, but just fine. Come on, I've fixed you some lunch."

They sat at the table. After they ate, Steven and Anne put the dishes in the sink. Having that done; Anne went over to the couch, propped her crutches against the wall, and laid on the couch. Steven came over and sat next to her. He leaned over and kissed her, as her arms went around his neck. He took his shoes off and lay beside her. She took her pants leg at the knee and pulled it up on her thigh, exposing her stump. Steven once again took hold of it and gently rubbed it. They laid together on the couch for hours. After a long while, Steven put his hand on her breast. She gently pulled his hand off as she shook her head.

"I've never been with a man, and I'm not quite ready yet. You know, I'm thirty-five years old. I must be at least ten years older than you. Things have not been easy for me since my accident. I haven't had a steady boyfriend since. As you can see, I'm no raving beauty. Steven, if I had to lose my leg, why couldn't I have been a beautiful woman? I have had a lonely life. I still hope the right man for me will come along." There was a tear in her eye, as she said this.

"It's very possible that he will, Anne, don't give up!" Steven said.

They played together all afternoon, and Steven invited her to come up to Grape Arbor and visit him at his mother's house during the holiday in February. She told him that she would think it over and let him know.

With a parting kiss, he left, gathered his belongings from his hotel, and caught his bus for Grape Arbor.

During the trip home he had an opportunity to give a lot of thought to what had happened over the past two days. Steven came to the conclusion that what he and Anne had done was neither strange, nor weird nor odd. Some might even consider there to be a certain amount of beauty in their actions. It was actually a form of communication. To Anne, her stump was her greatest problem. To her it was ugly, and she thought it made her unattractive. In her mind, her amputation was the stumbling block that was keeping her from the normal romantic experiences she really desired. She held no hope of obtaining them. She felt that her limp alone was enough to keep her from the interest of many men. For a very long time now she had believed that no man could want her because she was missing a leg. When Steven and Anne removed her leg and she placed her stump where Steven could fondle it, a communication started between them. Steven, by fondling her stump, began to deal with her fears. He was telling her that this leg indeed would not come between them. To him, she was all right. To him, she was as physically whole as any woman he had ever seen. He was saying with his gentle massage, it's all right Anne. Anne's and Steven's minds met on common ground, and they fit together physically as a hand in a glove. For the first time Anne began to wonder, was her impossible actually possible? Even for her?

Steven found, over the years, that almost all of the amputees that he had ever known intimately and often more casually, liked to be touched on their stumps. Many of them enjoyed it immensely, while others allowed it with the thought of pleasing him. This included about twelve women over the years. In all of that, time Steven met only one woman that did not want to be touched. For this reason Steven believed that it was a normal practice. He also believed that most of the women received a good deal of pleasure from it.

The current happenings in this book are set in 1959. The event that Steven is about to relate occurred in 1962, when Steven was a traveling salesman.

Steven was sitting at a blackjack table in a gambling casino in Nevada. He was uncharacteristically lucky that evening. As he was betting his hand, a pair of crutches were placed against the table next to him. When he looked across to the next seat, he saw a very attractive blonde seated there. He continued to play for several minutes until the lady accidentally dropped one of her chips on the floor. Steven got up to get her chip. When he did, he saw but one high heel shoe attached to a very long shapely right leg, resting comfortably on the floor. It appeared to Steven that she had no knee under her dress, on the left side. Steven returned with the chip and started a conversation with her. She was from back east and would return by plane on the next day. She had been visiting friends in a nearby town and decided to stop there for a day or so on the way home. It would be a chance to get a rest, and be alone for a while.

They seemed to be growing tired of the blackjack game. She told Steven her name was Kristen. Steven told her his name and offered to buy her a drink. She accepted then stood up, grabbed her crutches, and moved smoothly along side him. They crossed the street to a little bar in another casino. They sat in a secluded spot to the rear of the bar. Steven ordered drinks. As the were waiting for the drinks, Kristen volunteered the fact that she was hit by a car running a red light at the age of ten. She did not volunteer anything else of significance about herself. She did not want to discuss her life outside of this town. Steven honored her wishes.

The drinks came and they held hands under the table. Kristen was holding Steven's hand in such a way that it was lying across the top of her left thigh. When the second round of drinks came, Steven freed his hand and placed it on top of her dress over the end of her stump. She smiled politely. She was not distressed. She put the palm of her hand on his forearm, and gently rubbed in a circular motion. Steven moved his hand in a rubbing motion. Her face flushed, and she said quietly, "Oh! My! Oh! I've never had it happen like that before." Steven slid his hand under her dress and cupped the end of her leg. She blew a breath through her nose with a loud whomp. She said, "Steven, let's go to your room." Steven nodded with a grin, and paid the bar bill.

When Steven opened the door, the little swimming pool in the middle of the front room came into view. When Kristen saw the pool her eyes lit up. She went over to the bed and laid her crutches on it. As Kristen began to disrobe, he went to the other side of the bed and took his clothes off. He went around the bed and put his arms around her. They embraced for several minutes. Steven picked her up and sat her gently on the edge of the pool, her leg up to her knee in the water. He got into the pool and, for first time, marveled at the beauty of her breasts.

After they were in the pool for about an hour, Steven got towels for them. He helped Kristen out of the water. She stood, as he dried her off. When they had both dried off, they went to bed.

The next morning, Steven drove Kristen over to her hotel before driving her to the airport. That was the last Steven ever saw of Kristen. He had often wondered why she was so secretive. He thought that she might be facing some very serious problems at home.

The bus stopped and Steven walked to where he and his mother lived. Steven returned to school and found no more satisfaction with it than he had previously. He began drinking a little more. More than occasionally now, Steven would call Cynthia when he was drunk. He was still pining for Herta, and Cynthia tried her best to soothe him. Through correspondence, Steven and Anne agreed to have a visit at his mother's house during the February holiday. Anne stipulated that if she came up, Steven must promise to be good. Steven wasn't exactly sure what she meant, but he promised.

Steven met Anne at the bus depot. They had supper in the depot cafe, then walked the few blocks to the house. Steven's mother was still at work, so Anne and Steven went in and sat on the couch. They talked about her trip to Grape Arbor, and generally about school and work.

There were two couches in the front room. Steven and Anne decided that they would sleep in the front on the two couches. His mother would sleep in the bedroom where Steven usually slept. When his mother got home, she said that Anne would take the back bedroom. By midnight everyone was tired and decided to turn in.

About three in the morning, Steven awoke, finding that he had to go to the bathroom. On the way back, he found that Anne's door was slightly ajar. He looked in and saw her lying spread eagle on her stomach under the covers. Steven was surprised to see her lying in this position. He went to the room and slid under the covers beside her. When she discovered he was there, she rolled over and put her knee on his navel. He reached up her pant leg and caressed her stump. They held each other in an embrace and remained together for the rest of the night.

It was at this point that, for the first time, Steven made a serious effort toward making it with Anne. She resisted. She enjoyed being in bed with Steven, but she resisted his advances. Steven lightly pursued her. On the second morning when they woke Anne rolled over and gave him her stump once more.

She asked him, "Do you have anything to protect me?"

Steven reached to his night stand and produced a box of condoms. "Here, will this do the trick?"

Anne took one out of the box, looked at it, and gave it back to him. Steven put them back in the drawer. They lay together for another little while, then Anne got up, put her leg on, and went to the bathroom. When she returned, she took her leg off and got back in bed. She lay with her back to Steven.

Without really thinking about it, Steven realized that Anne was unbuttoning the bottoms of her pajamas. Steven put his hand on her bare hip. He slid it down past her stomach and rested it on her vulva. Steven, removed his bottoms, took the rubbers from the top drawer, and put one on. He rolled over on his side. After a few minutes, Anne rolled over on her back, and Steven removed her bottoms. She opened her top to allow Steven access to her breasts. Steven played gently with them for a bit. He then climbed between her thighs and gently rubbed the end of her leg as he penetrated her.

They stayed together another day, then Anne had to return to Southland.

Steven and Anne met one last time in Southland, only a few days after they were together in Grape Arbor. Steven didn't have very much money, so he hitchhiked to Southland. He met Anne in front of the elevators on the floor on which she worked. Steven told Anne that he needed some condoms. She told Steven that there was a drug store on the ground floor of the building. Steven was a bit surprised when she went in with him to get the rubbers. It was evident that Anne knew the druggist.

Steven gave some thought to the fact that she went into the drug store with him. It was no problem at all. He realized that Anne wanted to show somebody in the world that she also could have a boyfriend. She wanted people to know that she was just as able as anyone. When they got home, Anne insisted that Steven help her move her bed into the front room so that they could sleep together. When they finally went to bed, Anne suggested that Steven should sleep on her bed and she would sleep on the couch. With all this effort by Anne to be able to sleep together, Anne refused to sleep nude.

Steven didn't give a very good explanation to Anne. He knew that Anne was not the right woman for him. She could never be the missing piece. He felt badly about this, but he just knew it. He still missed Herta. He knew that Anne could not make that hurt go away. For one thing, she was very poor, not only from a financial stand point, but also poor in spirit. The real problem was not in her, however, but in Steven. At this point he had no faith in ever being able to find a job. He could not see how he could possibly ever be able to support her. He knew that he didn't love her. He also knew that at this point in time, he needed someone that he could lean on. He needed someone that could straighten him out. Together they were not rich enough to stay together. Steven wrote to Anne to this effect. Within a few days, Steven received a small package in the mail. It was what was left of the condoms.

Steven received a letter from a stranger shortly after this trip informing him that Barbara Chein had succumbed to her illness. He was very upset about this because, although they never met, he had every intention of meeting her. The timing was never right for them. That afternoon, at a meeting of the English Club, he paid tribute to Barbara by eulogizing her to the group. It may have been a little awkward, but Steven had to get it off his chest.

Steven found himself quite depressed. After getting very drunk that night, Steven called Cynthia and told her his woes. He said that he wanted to come and visit her in Missouri. She told him to come ahead. Steven, with no money, started to hitchhike. He caught a ride. By morning he was halfway to Southland. When the morning sun got into his eyes, he had a hangover. His head pounded and his guts ached. He was in no condition to go on. He knew that he was finished and returned to Grape Arbor even more depressed.

Steven was taking a very simple English class. It was, however, a required class for graduation. On that Monday morning, he was met at the entrance to the classroom by his teacher and the head of the department. It was early in the quarter and the class had hardly gotten started.

Dr. James spoke. "Steven, you are going to flunk this class!"

"What do you mean I'm going to flunk? The class has hardly begun."

"You are failing."

"How can you say that. We have had one assignment, and yet I'm failing? All we had to do was to fill out a number of file cards with famous quotes from literature."

Dr. James replied, "That's right, and you filled in the fewest number of cards. Therefore, you are getting the lowest grade which is F."

"Bull shit, Doctor. You just want to get rid of me because you do not think that I am a good candidate to be an English teacher. I'll admit to that, but might I remind you that I came here on your insistence that I could become a drama teacher if I came here. I would like to know where in the hell your curriculum for that is. Well, Doctor?"

"You've got me on that!"

There was no use in Steven's hanging around. "I will withdraw from school tomorrow. One last thing, you take this department and shove it."

That night, sinking deeper into depression, Steven went to a local bar and got drunk. He was depressed when he started drinking. By the middle of the evening he was so completely overwrought that he was crying profusely. He was sitting over in the corner of the bar, and no one was paying any attention to him. He began to think of the women that had been in his life. Now, it wasn't the up sides of them he was thinking about. He thought of the way they each had suffered. He thought of the fact that, not only had they each lost an important part of themselves, but they also lost what to them must have been a part of their beauty. As he was thinking, a half empty glass spilled and the contents made a waterfall of beer suds enroute to the floor. Steve thought of how clumsy he was and continued his pondering.

That was just a part, there must have been a great deal of

pain in the loss of the leg, at the beginning. Phantom pains were very common to most amputees. Then there came, for most a prothesis. This was a wooden caricature of a leg in which was encased the remains of a limb. The fit was so tight that the stump had no room to breath. Even when it was not hot weather the sweat poured off the end of the stump and filled the bottom of the socket. If a person did not wear a prosthesis, he or she then ran a high risk of falling and seriously injuring the most vulnerable part of the body. Perhaps for the first time, Steven felt sorry for them. He hurt for them. Right now, it was so deep, that he was in pain for them. Steven truly had a very deep identification. Ever since he was a little boy and had crawled into the closet to imitate his grandfather, for some reason, he felt that he really wanted to know. He questioned each of the women he came to know, in an effort to try to understand how it felt to have a missing limb. None of them could come anywhere close to giving him that understanding. His life was at a pretty low ebb right then. He was a twenty-four-year-old man with nothing.

Steven had the attitude about himself that he had no fear of losing a limb. The thought did not terrify him in anyway. It must be realized that Steven could not very well deal with these women if he had in himself a great fear of having an amputation. His attitude about the women he knew, and his attitude toward himself were strictly compatible.

Steven needed a change in his life. He had no desire to kill himself, but perhaps he could make himself into the person he wanted to be.

Suddenly he jumped up, grabbed his jacket, and raced out to his car. He put it in gear and raced down the city streets at sixty miles an hour, as if all hell was after him. When the car stopped, he found himself at the railroad station. He got out of his car and walked out onto the tracks. He picked a track, on which he thought the cars would be moving soon. He laid down next to the track and put his left leg under the wheel of the boxcar. For the first time in his life, he had no inhibitions. Nobody gave a damn about him anyway. It really didn't make any difference. He stayed there for two hours. Nothing moved, so Steven got up. Having sobered up a bit, he went home. He was convinced that he would not have moved his leg if the train came.

The next day, Steven went to his doctor and begged for help. He was still disappointed that the train did not move. Too many things were going wrong for him to handle. Everything had turned to shit. The doctor said that being that he had no money, the best solution would be to go the state mental institution. The doctor assured him that he would get treatment there. The doctor hated to see Steven tear up his life and suffer as he was. The doctor arranged for a court committal for Steven. The case would be heard on the next afternoon.

Steven didn't wait until evening to get drunk. He went to town with a snoot full. Wandered the streets of the town. He entered an ice cream parlor in the middle of town. As he entered the men's restroom he fell against the mirror behind the lavatory and broke it. He broke into tears. He could not contain the shame he felt because of the mirror. He came out of the restroom and told one of the soda jerks. The soda jerk told him that it was all right, and Steven left the place. Steven went home and passed out on his bed. He woke in a pool of tears.

The next afternoon, his doctor met him at the court house. They went before the judge, and the doctor told him that Steven was volunteering for court committal to a state mental hospital. The judge asked the reason for this action, and when the doctor declined to give an answer, the judge gave the order. Steven was taken into custody at that time.

The next day, at day break, Steven was taken from his overnight cell, and driven to the airport. He was handcuffed into a three seated Cessna. The other passenger was going to a minimum security prison further south. Steven thoroughly enjoyed the flight. When the plane landed, Steven was freed of his cuffs, and they hustled him into a black van with the name of the hospital in large white letters on its sides.

They eventually, came to a dusty road which lead to a high white wall through which they drove. As soon as they passed the wall, a heavy brown wooden gate swung closed behind them. A man could be seen bolting it shut out the back window of the van. It felt to Steven at that moment that the closure was very permanent.

For the first time Steven began to realize that he had relinquished all of his freedom. He no longer had any control over his present, or his future. He had no idea how long he would have to stay there. Indeed, he did not know if he would ever be allowed to leave. He only knew that he needed help desperately because he was constantly suffering. He did not know whether or not they could, or would, help him. He was desperate, and he had no desire to waste his life. The gate man, locked the gate.

Steven had lost his wife. He had no job. He was no longer in school. He had no money. There seemed to be nothing left to build on. At twenty-five Steven was too young to come to naught.

Steven did not find an end to his problems, nor was this the beginning. This was really round one. This experience created more questions than answers. Steven left Grape Arbor behind for good. He would never live there again. There is more to come, this is the middle.

There is a time to run, and a time to stop.
There is a time to learn, and a time to give up.
There is a time to listen, and there is a time to say bull shit.